LEVEL 7

LEVEL 7

MORDECAI ROSHWALD

Afterword by H. Bruce Franklin

LAWRENCE HILL BOOKS

First published by William Heinemann, Ltd., London
Copyright © William Heinemann, Ltd., 1959

Copyright © 1989 by Mordecai Roshwald
Printed in the United States of America
First Edition
First Printing
Published by Lawrence Hill Books
An Imprint of Chicago Review Press, Inc.
814 North Franklin Street
Chicago, Illinois 60610
ISBN 1-55652-065-4

LC# 89-15217

Cover design by Fran Lee

To George and Mikhail

ACKNOWLEDGMENT

My thanks are due to Jonathan Price
for translating the original manuscript
from my English into English and for
making many valuable suggestions.

INTRODUCTION

How I started to write this diary

Some time has passed—thirty-seven days, to be precise—since I decided to write this diary and started to do so. It seems longer: these thirty-seven days have stretched out like eternity. My previous life passes before my mind as a recollected dream, a remote image, the life of another man. In a way, I got adjusted to my new life pretty quickly, though I am still far from feeling happy.

It is now, when my diary is already quite substantial, that it occurs to me that it should have some sort of introduction.

Introduction for whom? I ask myself. What chance is there that the diary will ever see daylight? I mean that literally. For, my unknown and uncertain reader sometime in the future, this diary is being written in dungeons.

These dungeons are so deep underground that there is not the slightest chance of any ray of natural light penetrating into them. Not that we need daylight, of course. Our light down here is as strong as is desirable. It is scientifically adjusted to suit human needs. In some ways it is more perfect than sunlight: we get no gloomy days down here, and we never need sun-glasses. I'm told the temperature too is scientifically regulated—to 68 degrees, I believe. This must be the only place in the world where nobody ever talks about the weather. There isn't any.

So here I am, 4,400 feet down inside the earth, with no chance of seeing sunshine again, writing a diary which probably no one will ever read. The idea of writing it occurred to me a few hours after I had come down. They were very hard hours—hours in which I realised that I shall never go back

1

up to live on the surface of the earth again. But I must go back a bit to tell you how it happened.

The time was 8.00 a.m. and the date was March 21. I was sitting in my room at the PB (Push-Button) Training Camp. I had just had my breakfast, and I was in the act of glancing through the day's work-programme when there came a knock at the door. A messenger poked his head in and said that the Commanding Officer wanted to see me at once. I glanced in the mirror, flicked a speck of dust off the sleeve of my uniform, took my cap down from the peg behind the door, and left the room.

I had no idea I was walking out of one life and into another. I didn't even wonder much what the C.O. wanted to see me about. He quite often called one in without any advance warning. Sometimes it was for a fairly important matter—to say that you were to go on attachment to another training base, for example, or that you had been promoted, or that your work was not up to standard. Sometimes it was for one of his periodical inquiries about how you had spent your leave or week-end pass, to find out whether you had met anybody who seemed to be too interested in military secrets. And sometimes he called you in for a friendly-seeming chat without any apparent purpose, which made you wonder for the rest of the day whether he had had a hidden motive or was just plain bored and wanted somebody to talk to.

For the C.O. often was bored—lonely, anyway. As the administrative apex of a highly trained unit of military technicians, he was our superior in rank but inferior to us in technical education, in I.Q. and—so we thought—in his indispensability for modern warfare. So he was always obeyed, but seldom respected; and never treated as a friend. Our attitude probably resembled that of a bunch of privileged officer-cadets under a veteran sergeant who ruled as a god on the parade ground but with whom they would not have dreamt of associating in private. I wouldn't know for certain,

2

because I never was an aristocrat and our instruction bore little resemblance to the old-time training for officers.

To get back to my story: when I was summoned to the C.O. that morning I had no idea what to expect. I thought vaguely that it might be something to do with my leave. For the last three months I had not been allowed off the camp—it had been the final phase of my training period. I had not even had a week-end away. I felt I deserved some leave. We had excellent facilities for leisure inside the camp, but even the inconveniences of life outside seemed attractive once in a while. Now that I am deep underground, even the restricted life of the camp seems almost unbearably attractive in retrospect. And as for a week-end free to go where I liked and do what I wanted—I daren't think about it.

Anyhow, the notion that leave might be in store for me put me in a cheerful frame of mind as I walked over to the administrative block and entered the C.O.'s office. The C.O. was as quiet and controlled in his manner as ever, perhaps— so it seems to me now—even quieter and more controlled than usual. He asked me to take a chair, and then told me that the report on my final training was quite good. I was to be promoted to major, and would receive the increased pay which went with the rank. "As a matter of fact," he added with a superior smile, "you'll be getting rather more than I get, because of your technical qualifications." I thanked him for the news, and thought how cleverly he camouflaged his feeling of inferiority.

"Now, your leave," he went on, and my hopes rose. "Unfortunately," and he paused on the word, conscious of having scored, "that will have to be postponed for a day or two. You have been ordered down."

This meant underground, to the deep military installations of whose existence we trainees were, of course, aware, but which we had never seen.

"You'll be able to gain first-hand knowledge of those matters with which your training up here has made you ac-

3

quainted. And then," with his sweetest smile, "you will be truly capable of fulfilling your duty and repaying your country for the money, time and energy it has invested in you."

I swallowed that remark too. Coated, as it was, with the sweet sugar of higher rank and pay, it went down fairly easily.

"After you return from the trip down," the C.O. concluded, "you will go on two weeks' leave. This is a part of the order from above, which even I could not change if I wished to." He could never say a pleasant thing without some bitter twist; but it did not worry me. I was already thinking about my leave—my *ordered* leave.

Did the C.O. know that this leave business was only a trick, part of the routine for taking me, and my fellows, *smoothly* down? I do not think so. He was just passing on orders which he, just then, understood as little as I did.

When I asked him at what time I was expected to leave, he told me that a car was already waiting for me outside his office. This struck me as rather unusual, for normally an order of this sort allowed some time for personal preparation. Still, one purpose of a military training is to accustom you to obeying orders without asking questions. I therefore accepted without query another curious fact: that I should take nothing with me, not even a toothbrush. "Everything will be provided on the spot," said the C.O. "Just get into the car and go."

This was becoming interesting. But there was no time for meditation. I stood up, saluted, left the office, stepped into the waiting car, and we were off. I remember glancing at my watch. The time was 8.30.

It was not until a few days later, after my destiny had been made known to me, that I understood the reason for this haste. The Supreme Command wanted to take no chances. It did not want the men and women who were ordered down to talk to anybody who was to remain. They had to be taken down directly, without any contact with friends and relations. The

4

only man who knew that we—myself and some others from my camp—were going down was the C.O., and he could be relied upon to keep his mouth shut. Even the toothbrush I left had a function to fulfil. It would serve as evidence that my disappearance was purely accidental and unrelated to any military task. If I had been sent somewhere on duty, I would surely have taken my toothbrush with me. In short, my companions and I had to vanish as inconspicuously as possible, as if the earth had opened and swallowed us up. Which is precisely what happened.

The car in which I was being driven was a closed military model of unremarkable appearance, the type of car which might have been used by anybody from a lieutenant to a general. I was sitting by myself in the rear seat, feeling most comfortable. I clearly remember this sensation of comfort, because it occurred to me that this was the way a major *should* feel. I realise now how silly I was to let the business of my new rank fill my mind at that moment. But, reclining on the soft seat, I felt like Napoleon after Austerlitz.

After day-dreaming pleasantly for an hour or so I began to look more closely at one feature of the car which *was* unusual: a partition which divided the front and rear of the car into separate compartments. I remembered seeing old films in which taxi-drivers were often separated from their patrons by glass windows. But the partition in my car was made of some opaque plastic stuff. I could not even see the driver, let alone talk to him. I had no way of communicating with him, which was a pity, because I would have liked to ask him the reason for the partition. Presumably that is exactly why the screen was there: to stop me asking questions. Well, one gets used to that in military life. I sat back again and, for lack of anything better to do, gazed out of the car window in an effort to establish where we were going.

I did not learn much. We seemed to have left the signposted public roads, and were travelling across barren territory which I had never seen before.

At about 11.00 a.m. the car entered a tunnel. I just had time to notice how well the entrance had been camouflaged —the countryside was rocky, and two huge natural boulders formed an arch which quite hid the mouth of the tunnel— before we were inside and travelling down a steep but smooth and well-lit incline. The tunnel was wide enough for two cars to pass, but no vehicles were coming the opposite way. (I assume they must have used a special exit tunnel. In case of emergency, either of them could be used for two-way traffic.) My car had slowed down now, presumably because of other cars ahead of us which I could not see from my seat. Then it stopped, moved on and stopped again several times, as in a traffic jam. Suddenly—it did seem sudden, though I had been anticipating the moment—the car stopped again and the door was quickly opened by someone outside. This was it. I stepped out.

The car had drawn up very close to an entrance in the wall of the tunnel. There was only one way for me to go—through that entrance. A notice on the wall of the short passage in which I found myself read: 'Don't Stop! Keep Moving!' I passed through another door and entered a lift.

It was a fairly big one, about twelve feet square. Some people were in it already, and others were following me in. When it was quite full the door closed and down we went. As far as I could judge by the initial acceleration, the lift was travelling pretty fast—1,000 feet or more per minute. And as it took us about three minutes to reach our destination, I guessed we must be at least 3,000 feet undergound. As I learned later, it was even more than that: our dungeons were located 4,400 feet below the crust of the earth.

We stepped out into a well-illuminated corridor, some seven feet wide by seven feet high and twenty or thirty yards long. It was quite bare except for painted signs on the walls telling whoever was in it to proceed—hardly necessary, as the lift-door had closed firmly behind us. At the far end of the corridor was a revolving door through which we passed one

6

by one. I remember glancing behind me after I had gone through and noticing that one half of the door was blocked on the inside. And the door only revolved one way. But the full significance of this did not strike me at the time.

The passage in which we now found ourselves led to a moving staircase—only *one* such staircase, and moving *down*. A minute or so later I was standing in a long, narrow room which stretched about fifty yards on either hand. It was set at right angles to the escalator we had just come down. The escalator exit door was in the centre of one side of the room, and to its left and right were other doors spaced along the length of the wall. Each door bore an inscription of some sort, but I was more interested in examining the long table which ran the length of the other long wall, opposite the doors. It was supported by brackets from the wall, and at each extremity it appeared to run into a hole in the end wall of the room.

Before I had had time to examine it closely a woman's voice, very calm and clear, began repeating over a loudspeaker: "Everybody proceed to the table and be seated on the bench. Move along the room and do not block the entrance. Do not stop at the centre; move along the table. Thank you."

Soon the bench was filled to capacity, and no more people were coming in from the staircase. I could not count how many were seated at the table, but I guessed the number must be somewhere between 150 and 200 (I found out later that meals were in fact served to 177 or 178 persons at a time). Then the voice on the loudspeaker was heard again: "Attention, please! Lunch will be served presently."

Whereupon, as if at an agreed signal, everybody started talking. Though my neighbours were perfect strangers to me, they addressed me and I addressed them at almost the same moment.

"Well, that *was* a ride!" "So this is the bowels of the earth!" "We must be very deep down." "Thirty-five hundred feet, I'd say." "More than that!" "And quite quickly done." "I won-

7

der what we'll get for lunch." "I feel rather hungry after all that." "So do I." "Well, I don't."

Such were the things we said: not profound things or purposeful things, but somehow important to the people seated at the table. It was only after this spontaneous talk had erupted all along the line that it occurred to me that not a word had been uttered all the way down in the lift, along the corridors, on the escalator and finally in this dining-room. Apparently we had all been so preoccupied with the experience of going down that we had hardly noticed each other's existence. The intensity of our brooding was revealed only after the familiar idea of lunch had jerked us out of ourselves and set our tongues free.

Now the loudspeaker addressed us again: "Attention, please! Your lunches will be served to you on the moving band of the table. Wait till the band stops. Then start eating. Eat everything you are given. You will need it. Don't forget the pills: they are important for your diet. Don't wonder or hesitate about the food. It was scientifically prepared to meet the needs of men and women in this new environment. Thank you." Click.

Even before the loudspeaker had finished, the band had started to move, and I saw what the voice meant. I had not noticed before that the table was covered with a wide strip of some plastic substance which ran the whole of its length and into the slots in the end walls. As the band moved it bore dishes of food towards us from one of the holes. It moved smoothly and quite quickly, and slowed down steadily to a halt as the first dish reached the far end of the room. Now the long table was covered with identical, equally-spaced plates which—as I found when I tried—were attached to the band and could not be removed. Beside each place, on a magnetised metal disc, stood a metal cup which was further secured by a spiral wire to the plastic band. A medium-sized spoon was fastened to the band by a similar wire. In this way the cup and the spoon could be used but not taken away, on

8

exactly the same principle as the pencils provided for customers in some offices. The magnetic 'saucer' stopped the cup sliding about when the band was in motion and also, I guessed, held it firm when the endless band passed upside-down through a washing machine which cleaned table, crockery and cutlery all together. I found out later that my guess had been right, and that the whole process, including doling out the food, was fully automatic.

The food—well, that was rather disappointing. If we hardly found time to say so, it was because we were so busy talking about the other astonishing arrangements. There was very little to eat on the plate, and it had hardly any taste; but somehow it managed to satisfy our hunger. It consisted of a small piece of reddish stuff (some sort of synthetic multi-purpose food) which was eaten with the spoon, and three pills. The pills one washed down with the half-pint or so of yellow liquid contained in the cup.

I do not know why I am going into such detail about all this. Probably because my first impressions of the underground arrangements were particularly sharp. It quite often happens that on momentous occasions we pay most careful attention to the least significant facts. This first meal has been preserved in my mind as a memorable event, a sacrament initiating me into this holy of holies—or rather, into this hole of holes.

As soon as we had eaten our meal—which did not take long —and the band had carried our plates and cups into the other slot in the wall, the loudspeaker sounded again. We were ordered to go each to his respective department. The door to each section was clearly marked, and I soon found one saying 'Push-Button X'. In the course of looking for my door I noticed the inscriptions on some of those which the other men and women were entering: 'Hospital M', 'Administration Ad', 'Air Supply AS'. However, I had no time to examine all the doors. Trained to respond alertly, I turned at once into 'Push-Button X'.

9

After passing through a narrow corridor, which had one door on each side, I went through another door at the end into what I recognised at once as the Push-Button X Operations Room. There was nothing strange about this room. It was exactly the same as the one back up there in the training camp. I won't bother to describe it now, because I have already done so elsewhere in the diary.

In the Operations Room there was already another man waiting. He wore a uniform like mine, was of about the same age and build, and seemed somehow familiar—possibly because I had seen him before somewhere, possibly because he seemed to resemble me so much. Before we could say anything the door opened and two more men came in one after the other. I recognised one of them—a fellow-trainee from the PB camp—and the other one appeared to know the man who had been there when I arrived. (I learnt later that they had trained together at another PB camp.)

We had no time to introduce ourselves before a loudspeaker addressed us: "Attention, gentlemen! As you see, you are in the Push-Button X Operations Room. You are collectively and individually responsible for this room. This room must never, repeat never, be left unattended.

"Now, let me introduce you to one another. The gentleman near the door is Push-Button Officer X-117; on his right stands X-137; the officer in the centre of the room is X-127; the fourth is X-107, and he is the first on duty. He will be relieved at 18.00 hours by X-117. However, he must not leave the Operations Room until his relief has actually arrived.

"The others may now retire to their rooms. X-117 and X-137 will occupy the room located on their right as they re-enter the corridor from this room. X-127 will occupy the room on the left-hand side, together with X-107.

"Thank you, gentlemen!"

It seemed that our manœuvres were to be just like the real thing: lodgings near the Operations Room, one man always on duty—a perfect exercise, I thought. At the time it did not enter my head that—well, I found out before very long.

We must have appeared on the viewing screen of the unknown person who had introduced us through the loudspeaker, but the thought did not embarrass me. I shook hands with my comrades-in-buttons, exchanged friendly greetings with my fellow-trainee, X-137, and spoke a few polite words to X-107, the one remaining on duty.

The combined living- and bed-room which I now entered surprised me by its smallness. It looked very much like the tiny cabin I had once seen illustrated in a book on military history, in the days before ships became obsolete as an arm of military operations, along with tanks and aircraft. Of course, it was electronic equipment which had crowded out those old sailors. And I decided it must have been the sheer sweat of building *anything* down here which accounted for the fact that this bed-living-room was made so small.

A pair of bunks, one above the other, occupied most of the space. There was one ordinary chair and another seat which pulled down on a hinge from the wall if a second person wanted to sit down. There was also a desk which worked on the same principle. Under the lower bunk there were several drawers which, to my surprise, were filled with neatly folded uniforms, shirts, underclothes and so forth. Also some writing materials. A door led into a little bathroom, the equipment of which—an excellent shower, wash-basin and toilet—compensated somewhat for the economies of the other room.

After exploring my new quarters I decided I would put my feet up for a while. I still felt excited, but the welter of new experiences had tired me. I took off my jacket and shoes, assigned the lower bunk to my companion and lay down on the top one. There did not seem to be anything else to do, anyway.

I do not know how long I lay there like that because I must have fallen asleep for a time. The next thing I remember is hearing a woman's voice, the one which had come over the

11

loudspeaker in the dining-room, repeat several times, loudly: "Attention please, attention! Attention please, attention!"

The voice was coming from a loudspeaker built into the ceiling of the room. I had not noticed it before. Lying on the top bunk, I had the sensation that somebody was holding me by the lobe of my ear and shouting into it to make sure I did not miss a word.

"Attention please, attention!" is still ringing in my head. Sometimes when I try to relax, take a warm shower, unharness my thoughts from my daily duties and let them loose on the sunny meadows of my terrestrial past, I suddenly realise that my lips are silently forming words. I speak them out loud, and always they are the same words: "Attention please, attention!"

I was lying wide awake now with my eyes open, ready to take in the message. It was very clear.

"Attention please, attention! This message is addressed to all underground forces on Level 7.

"You have been brought here today to serve as the advance guard of our country, our creed, our way of life. To you men and women on Level 7 is entrusted the operation of the offensive branch of the military machine of our country and its allies.

"You are the defenders of truth and justice. Our infamous and treacherous enemy has gone too far in developing his striking-power. In order to make ourselves safe from surprise attack and capable of retaliation, it is imperative that we protect our protectors, that we secure for our security forces the best possible shelter. That is the reason why you have been brought down to Level 7. From here you will be able to defend our country without the slightest chance of danger to yourselves. From here you will be able to attack without being attacked. To the world above you are invisible, but you hold the destiny of that world beneath the tips of your fingers. A day may come soon when some of you will be com-

12

manded to push a button, and your fingers will annihilate the enemy and make the victory ours.

"Till that day," the loudspeaker went on, "you will have to serve your country and humanity on Level 7. This is a privileged position, and you may feel proud to have been chosen for this duty. Remembering that this is also the safest place on earth, you may feel happy too. Arrangements have been made for every aspect of your well-being. You will have all you need. There is no danger of supplies running short: thanks to modern scientific achievements, we are self-sufficient here on Level 7. You need not worry about your friends and relatives outside. They will be notified that you have been killed in a painless accident and that you left no remains. We regret this, but your disappearance must remain absolutely secret. Down here you will find new friends and create new families.

"All this had to be done the way it was done, and we are happy to announce that Operation Level 7 Down, which brought you here today, was a complete success. Needless to say, there is no way back available to you; but it will please you to know that neither is there any way for radioactive pollution, should any occur, to find its way down here: the system was hermetically sealed as soon as the last of you had arrived this morning. You are safely cut off from the surface of the earth and from the other six shelter levels. We wish you and ourselves—for we are with you—good luck. Get adjusted to your new environment.

"Let us all get adjusted! Thank you."

The loudspeaker was silent. I lay on my bunk without moving a finger. I had heard every word of the announcement perfectly clearly, yet I was not as shocked as might have been expected. Maybe the blow was so severe that my feelings were somehow outshocked, pushed beyond the limits of normal reaction. Perhaps we had been given a sedative in our meal. Or it may have been some self-protective mechanism of the mind which worked as a buffer to guard it from the full emotional impact of the message it had intellectually understood.

So there I lay, quite still, knowing what the message had said, and yet perplexed. Was it my lack of reaction which puzzled me? Or was it some aspect of the message which I had not fully understood?

My eyes were wide open, fixed on the loudspeaker, and one sentence *was* echoing backwards and forwards in my head: "Till that day you will have to serve your country and humanity on Level 7. . . . Till that day you will have to serve your country and humanity on Level 7. . . . Till that day . . ."

Till *what* day? I began to ask myself. Till the day of victory, of course, as the message said. But what if there were no victory? What if the enemy were victorious?

Well, we stood at least a fifty-fifty chance of winning; probably better. And anyway, fighting soldiers had always had to lose some of their freedom, and had never fought in safer circumstances than those in which I found myself. The announcement had made it clear that Level 7 was the safest place on earth. If war happened, the chances of surviving outside would be nil. I knew quite well what atomic war implied. Even if *we* were victorious, the damage up on top would be so disastrous and the atomic pollution so widespread that no living creature could exist there. I was very lucky to be on Level 7.

But, my thoughts ran on, what if the war were postponed for five years, ten years, fifteen years? What if the war never happened? Should I have to spend the rest of my life in these dungeons, waiting for the command to press the buttons—a command that might never come?

"Till that day you will have to serve your country and humanity on Level 7."

Till when? Why didn't we start the war at once and get it

14

over with? Why wait? I desperately wanted to get out, the sooner the better.

It was then, as I lay there with my eyes still fixed on the loudspeaker, that the full truth of my situation went home like a knife in my back: whatever happened, I was down there for life. Even if we declared war that instant and won it inside a day, I would never be able to go back. The radioactive pollution caused by a full-scale atomic war would be such that the surface of the earth would be uninhabitable for decades. Perhaps for centuries.

I would never see it again.

I think I must have intuitively guessed this fact as soon as I heard the words of the announcement. Then I had felt puzzled because I had not worked out the logical steps that led from the words which came over the loudspeaker to the conclusion my mind jumped to. The jump had stunned me, so that I hardly felt anything.

But now I could feel. Now that I had worked out and checked the conclusion to which my guess had carried me, I could begin to appreciate what living down here would mean. I would never see towns again, or green fields. I would never walk down a street again, mixing with a crowd of people. And I would not see any more sunshine.

That was the thought that bothered me most. It made me nearly mad, the idea that I would never see sunshine again. Level 7 was worse than a jail, I thought, because even prisoners walked around a yard now and then, in the sunshine. I wanted to break out, to go up. At that moment I did not care *how* dangerous life on top might be. I wanted to live there and die there, under the sun, and not to decay slowly down in this miserable hole.

My mind was not coolly analysing the situation now, but boiling with hectic plans for escape. How could I get out? I *had* to get out. Then I remembered the escalator which moved only one way—down. At the head of it had been the revolving door which allowed no return. And beyond that was the lift-shaft, which must have been sealed off if what the loudspeaker had said was true. Even if I were able to race up those swiftly moving stairs and batter down the door, I would have no way of operating the lift. I could push a button to destroy the world, but there was no button I could push to summon that lift.

My frustration and despair had reached such a pitch that I was finding it impossible to lie still any longer. I had to get up and do something, anything to keep me busy. But what *could* I do? There were no books to read. I could not write a letter to anyone.

No, but I could *write!* I remembered the writing materials I had seen in the drawer. (A good psychological move on someone's part, that was.) I could write just for myself—a sort of diary of thoughts, feelings, impressions, things I did. And one day—who knows?—my diary might be discovered and published on the surface of the earth, up there in the sunshine. Part of me, my spirit, might one day see daylight, might be warmed by the sun!

I knew I was cheating myself. I knew that the chances of my diary's appearance up on the earth were remote. Even if the sun did shine on it one day, what good was that to me here and now? Still, I liked the illusion. It was comforting, even exciting. So I started writing this diary, and now whenever I sit down to report on another day, I have that same feeling of comfort and excitement.

I shall go on writing this diary as long as I live. For this is the only way in which I can feel the sun.

April 27.   X-127.

MARCH 21

Now I begin to understand the meaning of the problem 'to be or not to be'. Till now I only thought of being *somebody*. Earlier today I enjoyed the thrill of becoming a major,

16

of being somebody more exalted than I was yesterday. 'To be or not to be' seemed to me a vague, meaningless sort of question, good for philosophers or writers but of no interest to ordinary practical people. 'I am' was a simple fact, beyond any dispute just because it was a fact; whereas *what* I was might have been a problem, one of practical significance, because my rank, my social level, my health, any number of things about me were liable to change.

But the more I think about it, the more this idea of being, *pure* being, loses its simple form and collects around it other ideas. It begins to mean breathing fresh air, walking in the sunshine, and in the rain too—enjoying the sensation of existence.

Well then, is life down here *being*—or is it *not*-being? Is not Level 7 a sort of Hades or Sheol where being is dimmed to half-being, at the best? I can breathe, but is this fresh air? I can walk, but I cannot go for a walk. As for sunshine—I had better forget it. I feel that I feel, but I don't really—not in the spontaneous way I used to up there.

Am I condemned to half-be for the rest of my life? To half-be a *major*, to be sure. But I would rather revert to private and *be*. I would prefer to be an absolute nobody than to half-be what I am.

It is very odd that I had to be brought down into the depths of the earth in order to discover the meaning of half a line of Shakespeare. There must have been a philosopher, a Hamlet lurking in me all the time, and I never suspected it. I did not once ponder about the meaning of being, as long as I *was*. Now, when my life can hardly qualify as being, I begin to understand. . . .

Understand what? The meaning of being? Nonsense, nobody knows the meaning of that. But now at least I understand the meaninglessness of being *somebody*. And I realise the *significance* of being, without knowing what being is. My soul—what is left of it—cries: "To be, to be!"

But the loudspeaker sounds: "Attention please, attention."

17

Today I did my first spell of duty in the PB Operations Room. I shall have to be on duty for a total of six hours daily, as there are four of us and the room must be attended all round the clock. Nobody could call it hard work, certainly. It gets a bit boring, but you can have music there if you feel like listening. We have it in our rooms as well. Just push the right button, and out the music comes. There are only two programmes—one of light music and one of rather heavier stuff—but they seem inexhaustible. No tune has been played twice yet. It must all be recorded, of course—there is no room for live entertainers down here.

Still, I was about to describe the Operations Room. It is quite small really, though it is huge compared with our bed-living-room. There are only a few instruments in it, all of them familiar to me from my training.

On the wall is a big convex screen, a sort of flattened half-globe of the other side of the world, on which are mapped out the countries of our potential enemy and his satellites. It is lit in such a way that every part of it can be seen clearly by a person on duty in the room. On it are marked the enemy's points of strategic importance—strategic, not tactical. If push-button war is declared we shall not waste our time attacking points of temporary or local importance. Our blows will go straight to the heart and sinews of enemy territory. No tactical operations could be conducted from Level 7, anyway, and I cannot see any point in having them in a future war at all, unless it takes the ridiculously anachronistic form of limited hostilities.

The screen-map is divided into three zones, separated by thin lines. These zones have been determined by their distance from our rocket bases. The nearest one is called Zone A, the next one B, and the farthest one C.

There are two chairs in the room, equidistant from the screen and facing it at a convenient angle, one from the right and the other from the left. In front of each chair is a little table, and on each table stands what might be mistaken for a little typewriter or an adding-machine. In fact this gadget is the nucleus of the room and the sole reason for my being down here on Level 7.

On the gadget are three rows of four buttons. The front row, nearest the operator, covers enemy Zone A; the middle row Zone B; and the third row Zone C, the most distant. Each set of buttons controls a different type of destructive weapon —all of them long-range atomic rockets, of course. Buttons 1 control batteries of rockets with warheads the equivalent of one to five megaton bombs, which explode on touching the ground. This is an efficient means of destroying heavy and concentrated installations, military or industrial. The rocket-bombs controlled by the second set of buttons are much more powerful—ten to fifty megatons—and are designed to explode in the air, causing widespread destruction over big cities and heavily populated areas. Rockets of similar power, but constructed in such a way as to penetrate deep underground before exploding, are released by Buttons 3. The effect of these would be rather like that of an earthquake as far as destruction on the surface goes, and they would severely damage underground installations. Also they would produce a fair amount of lethal radiation, but this is more specially the task of the rockets controlled by the fourth set of buttons. These are 'rigged' atomic bombs; that is to say, bombs which are cased in a shell made of a potentially highly radioactive element. The bursting of the bombs would pulverise these shells into a fine, pervasive and strongly radioactive dust. This kind of weapon, which destroys life not only by heat, blast and shock, but by radiation, is in a way the most deadly of all. Its effects may last for a long time.

Each of the twelve buttons would release several thousands of otherwise electronically controlled and guided missiles,

19

every one of them aimed at a pre-determined target. They would hit the enemy within anything from fifteen minutes to an hour from when the button was pushed.

All this may sound rather complicated, but it is really very simple. My 'typewriter' looks like this:

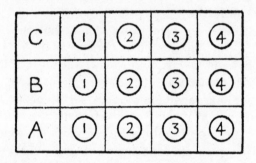

As a matter of fact, it is not all that important to know exactly what the buttons do, because the orders would be quite explicit: 'Push Button A1', or 'Push Button B3', or 'Push Button C2'. It is not certain whether Buttons 4 would actually be used. Some people have said they might prove dangerous even to the country using them.

All kinds of orders come through the loudspeaker; but to indicate that a push-button order is on the way there is in addition a visual warning system. First, a yellow lamp above the screen would light up to alert us. Then, a red lamp, if the yellow one was not a false alarm; and as soon as the red light came on we could expect our orders.

As a precaution against any officer who might push a button by accident, or because he had taken leave of his senses, or for any other reason, the system will only work if two people push the same button at the same time. This is the reason for the second chair, table and identical control box in the Operations Room. The two controls are far enough apart to stop one man pushing both the buttons at once. In case of emergency a second officer will be summoned into the room, and the two men will together execute the orders which come from the loudspeaker, sanctioned by the red light.

The two officers will be able to watch the results of their actions. As I said, the enemy targets are marked on the screen. If Button A1, say, is pressed, off go the one-to-five megaton rocket-bombs to Zone A in the enemy's territory. Their release will be signalled by the appearance of red points in the little circles on the map which show the appropriate Zone A targets. When the rockets actually hit their targets the red marks will expand to cover the areas destroyed. If they should fail to reach the targets—because of interception by the enemy, or some accident—then the red points will disappear again.

Buttons 2, 3 and 4 produce similar effects, in blue, yellow and black respectively.

Obviously the idea is to use the less destructive rockets first, and to resort to those causing widespread damage and death later on if the more limited weapons prove ineffective. However, my colleagues and I do not decide when to push the button, or which one to push. Our job is just to keep watch and, if and when the time comes, to do what the loudspeaker tells us. Our potential productive work is limited to the pushing of twelve buttons, twelve keys in a peculiar sort of typewriter. When we have done this our country's arsenal of offensive weapons will have been exhausted; but the other half of the world will have been completely destroyed.

MARCH 23

"Why the hell did they pick me for training as a push-button officer? Why couldn't they choose somebody else? Our C.O. back in the camp, for example—he might have enjoyed it. Why pick on me?"

Apparently I must have spoken these thoughts out loud earlier this evening, for I received an unexpected answer—

21

from the loudspeaker. There must be a system of supervision which enables the command to hear what we say even in the 'privacy' of our rooms.

The loudspeaker—it was a woman's voice—spoke softly: "You were chosen because of your personal qualities. You must have proved to be a man of stable disposition, technically skilful, ambitious, intelligent and very healthy. Also you must have got a very high score in claustrophobia tests."

That was all. The loudspeaker went silent again. I was eager to continue the conversation and asked some question, but I got no answer. Either the woman was laconically inclined, or she had to speak to someone else.

For a moment this event made me forget my meditations. Then I resumed them.

The woman was right: I *was* ambitious, and that was what had made me accept the offer of training. I was only a private at the time. Suddenly, after I had undergone (without in the least knowing why) a long series of medical, psychological and psychotechnical tests, I was offered immediate promotion to the rank of lieutenant, with excellent 'special' pay and allowances and prospects of further advancement after training. The job sounded attractive—it seemed to have something to do with gadgets, which I had always liked—and moreover it was stressed as being of the utmost importance. I jumped at it.

Perhaps if I were more sensitive I would have hesitated before signing a declaration which committed me to absolute secrecy about things which I was going to learn and whose nature was quite mysterious to me at the time. A more sensitive person might have been scared by the unknown; but I had scored very high in the test for emotional stability.

I dare say a more sensitive person would go mad living down here without a hope of getting out. So that is why they chose me! All right, but I do not consider that that is any guarantee that I shall not go mad myself.

I might be better off now if I had been just unstable enough to fail all those tests they gave me. Some people do not seem to mind the life down here, though. That woman on the loud-speaker sounds as if she takes it all in her stride.

MARCH 24

Today I had a nice talk with X-107, the comrade-in-buttons with whom I share my room. We had exchanged a few words before, of course; but I did not feel like entering into a lengthy conversation until today. I was too much preoccupied with my new situation. The idea that I was to stay on Level 7 for the rest of my days hammered in my head all the time, and other people—my neighbours at meals, my old fellow-trainee X-137, my new partner here in the room—seemed hardly to exist. I saw them as mere shades of the underworld, and made more contact—I might even say *social* contact—with the sheets of paper on which I was writing my diary. They were the intimate witnesses of my innermost feelings, the sharers of my new experiences. And because they seemed my only possible link with the outside world, I felt I was speaking through them to *real* creatures, men and women living under the sun.

Apparently my friend X-107 must have had similar feelings, for he was not inclined to talk either. Strange though it may seem, I do not remember hearing anyone discuss our predicament seriously before today. It seems that our plight did not create any quick, warm comradeship—the kind of fraternity which is supposed to spring up when, say, people are shipwrecked together. Instead there was a curious lack of interest in other people; perhaps even some resentment, as if each thought the others were responsible for his present state.

It goes without saying that everybody was clearly aware of the situation, even if they did not speak a word about it. You could tell they all knew by the general air of resignation: the

23

way they walked, ate their meals, and talked banalities if they talked at all.

Today, however, I was looking through my pages of diary when X-107 suddenly spoke, in a voice revealing some warmth, some sunshine from above: "Are you writing something?"

The direct, personal question and the friendly tone of his voice made me turn round from the desk and look him full in the face. For the first time I was really stirred to find out just what my room-mate looked like.

X-107 has an open and rather kind face, suggesting a man of quiet disposition, well-balanced and firm. He is perhaps a year or two older than I, which may be why I had a pleasant sensation as if I were talking to an elder brother when I answered his question: "Yes, I'm writing a diary. I found some writing-paper in the drawer here, and that gave me the idea. It's a sort of relief, you know!"

That broke the ice completely, and at once we started talking freely, as if we had known each other for years.

Oddly enough, he did not complain. He considered our service on Level 7 a necessity: unpleasant, true, but still an unavoidable development in view of the recent progress in military science. "To complain about our lot," he said, "is as futile and senseless as to complain about death. What one cannot escape one must accept; and the less fuss, the better."

I said something about dungeons, prison and solitary confinement. He said he had felt that way about our life down here, too, at first; but now he was beginning to understand how even imprisonment is not an absolute condition. "Some people," he said, "feel imprisoned when they can't travel through space. Others can feel free in a small room, if they are able to think or write." He smiled as he said this, and glanced at the sheets of paper lying on the desk, clearly implying that writing my diary might have this releasing effect.

I had admitted this already, in a way, by calling it a relief. And now, listening to his incisive, firmly stated arguments, I

24

was almost persuaded that I could come to feel about things in the same way that he did. It was comforting to hope that his way of thought might become mine.

Now I am not so sure that it ever will. I *want* to be able to feel the way X-107 feels, or thinks he feels, but this comes hard to me. Still, the knowledge that I am sharing a room with someone stronger than myself, someone who has found a way of adjusting himself to the new conditions, is in itself very comforting. I feel a little less lonely now, not so deep in despair. If a human being *can* get adjusted to the idea of spending his life on Level 7, then perhaps one day I shall get adjusted myself. If I cannot get out of here, at least let me have some sort of tolerable life as long as I live! If. . . .

No, maybe it is better not to 'if' too much. Let me look around, see what is happening, meet people, make friends, 'get adjusted'.

MARCH 25

Today I asked X-107 the question which has been worrying me all the time since my arrival on Level 7. The question of why we had to lose our freedom. I already knew some of the answers—they had been implied or stated in that initial announcement of our fate which I had listened to on my bunk four days ago—but I still wanted to talk the thing over.

"Why," I asked X-107, "were we condemned to life imprisonment down here? Couldn't we do our work on the surface of the earth? Hidden away in the middle of a desert, or something? Why here, so deep, so completely cut off?"

"Now you're talking like a child," he replied. "PBX Command had to be secured—secured absolutely—against surprise attack, an attack which might have hit us in your secluded desert hide-out just as fatally as in the centre of a metropolitan area. If it had, our country would have been knocked out without being able to fire back a single shot.

25

Down here on Level 7 we're safe from surprises like that. Even if the enemy destroys our country in a surprise attack, we—you and I—can retaliate and destroy *his* country."

"Still," I tried to argue, "even if PBX Command had to be located on Level 7, there was surely no need to *imprison* us here! Why can't we be relieved by other crews and go on leave every now and then?"

"That would be very dangerous," X-107 answered. "If you were able to get out, you might come back with a destructive weapon, or a destructive idea, which could put PBX Command out of action. Contact with the outside world could mean contact with spies, with enemies, with pacifists. The government would be foolish to take such a risk."

"So we had to be imprisoned for life in order to safeguard our country's powers of retaliation?"

"Exactly," he replied. "And to ensure its survival too: even if a surprise attack annihilates the population up above, down here we will go on living—after taking vengeance, of course."

I asked: "But what happens if there is no war?"

"Well," came the unperturbed answer of my room-mate, "our job is to be ready at all times to pull the trigger—to push the button. If no command to do so comes, we shall have served our country just the same; for if our enemy refrains from attacking us, it will only be because he knows how well prepared and unassailable we are down here on Level 7. So, on Level 7 we have to stay."

I could find no flaw in his argument. Our imprisonment on Level 7 is a necessity.

MARCH 26

My closer contact with X-107 is a help to me. We talk to each other about various things and this, sometimes, makes me forget my situation. Another thing that helps is the lounge which has been opened for everybody on Level 7.

The announcement came over the loudspeaker—this is the only way announcements and orders are made known—yesterday at noon. As the lounge is very small, like most rooms here, and the demand is expected to be considerable, each person has been allotted certain hours when he may use it. I say 'certain hours', but that is misleading. Half an hour each day. That is my ration, anyway.

The room *is* small for a lounge—about fifteen feet by twenty. It asserts its identity, though, by having its name painted bold and clear on the door, one of the many doors in the long wall of the dining-room. When I walked in, there were already some ten or fifteen people there, none of whom I remembered seeing before.

Some of them were women. They all seemed quite nice and looked young, strong and healthy, though I found none of them specially attractive. I went up to one who was standing by herself at the time, and introduced myself. She was a nurse, N-527.

What I liked about her was her calmness. I do not know how she managed it, but she seemed even more calm and relaxed than X-107. Perhaps women are more self-sufficient than men (provided they have men) and less affected by environment. If so I envy them—for the first time in my life.

After a while another man approached us, introducing himself as E-647, 'E' standing for Electrical Engineer. He was behaving rather nervously, and soon had me on edge too. I decided to look for other company and leave him to the nurse. I had the impression he was grateful for that.

For a moment I stood alone. Then another woman came up to me, possibly a little older than the nurse, though not over twenty-five. I learnt that she was a psychologist, P-867. She was another calm person, but her calmness seemed of a different kind—a bit artificial, as if she were proud of the achievement—rather than the calmness of a naturally serene disposition. As we talked this got on my nerves.

The first thing she said was, how did I feel? I did not feel inclined to confide in a person I had only just met. I evaded the question: said I was very busy and had had no time to analyse my feelings. She brushed this aside and promptly suggested that I was either deliberately lying or else trying to escape from reality. In either case, she maintained, my attitude was not healthy: "Face reality and talk to other people about your feelings. That's the best way to get adjusted."

Trying to escape her professional zeal, which made me feel like a laboratory guinea-pig, I asked her about her own feelings. "Oh," she said, "I feel fine." And she went on to explain why she felt so well. The experience of living on Level 7 was most interesting from the psychological point of view. She would have loved to undertake a piece of psychological research into the response of Level 7's crew to their new surroundings. (So I *was* a guinea-pig!) It would make a fascinating article if only she could publish the results of her research, which she obviously could not do on Level 7.

At that point I interrupted her: "So you too think in terms of 'if'?" She did not understand. I explained that *I* had been thinking in terms of 'if': *if* I had not been chosen for Level 7, *if* it were possible to go back up on leave, *if* I had the disposition of a woman. . . .

"You mustn't think in those terms," she protested. "That's escapism. You *must* find here and now what you *can* find here and now." It sounded like some kind of slogan. "Don't look backwards and don't think hypothetically. There's a lot of meaning in our life here. You have a job to do, a country to defend. You have human company here—even female company." And she suddenly giggled. "What more can a man want, tell me that?"

I answered, almost inaudibly: "Sunshine."

She remained quiet for a long while and then vigorously shook her head: "No. Sunshine can't in itself be a real need. I've studied quite a few psychological systems, and not one of them ever regarded the quest for sunshine as a basic motivation of human beings, or as a possible foundation for neurosis.

28

Definitely not. There must be some other reason for your state of mind. Sunshine is just a symbol. What lies *behind* that is the real cause."

At that moment the loudspeaker announced that our time in the lounge was up. As we parted outside the door she remarked: "You never know—one day you may need psychological treatment. I'll be happy to help you." At this she giggled again.

MARCH 27

I am trying to divert myself by learning what I can about the technical arrangements on Level 7. In their way they are pretty remarkable. This is a very small world, but it seems to be quite self-sufficient. Although it lies so deep underground it has its own supply of energy, food and all the other essential commodities needed by its crew. We might be on a ship, equipped for an endless voyage.

For one thing, we shall never run out of fuel. Everything here works by electricity from dynamos powered by an atomic reactor which can supply all the energy we want for a thousand years. There is nothing new in this principle, but when you think of all the gadgets which are using up electricity twenty-four hours a day down here you appreciate how impossible life would be without an atomic reactor.

The problem of storing nourishment must have been more complicated; but at dinner today somebody provided some interesting information about that. (People have started to be more talkative lately.) He said—and he appeared to know what he was talking about—that dehydrated food in enormous quantities is stored in a huge deep-freeze. At each meal the necessary amount is automatically taken out of the freeze, warmed, mixed with water and served on our plates. Being dehydrated, it takes up very little space. Even so, the storage

29

of enough to feed 500 people for 500 years is no simple matter.

The man's mention of 500 years made everybody fall silent for a few moments. I expect the others were thinking the same as I was. I sometimes feel as if I have been down here months already, not just days; and to think of Level 7 in terms of centuries is beyond my imagination.

One of the women made it her task to break the silence by asking how enough water could be stored underground. "There is no dehydrated water," she added, and was rewarded by a few bleak smiles from the rest of us.

However, we gathered from the expert that there is no need to store water, and that the supply is unlimited. In fact it is the only commodity which can never run short. It reaches us from deep underground sources, inexhaustible because of precipitation.

"At first," the expert said, "it was feared that the water might become contaminated in the event of an atomic war. Then it was found that the thick layers of earth through which the water has to pass on its way down act as excellent filters. We stand no risk of drinking impure water."

Our meal was nearly over, when somebody raised the question of refuse. The disposal of sewage and other rubbish on Level 7 was surely as big a problem as the storage of food.

But this problem too has been solved with great ingenuity. All the refuse is led through an ordinary drainage system into a special machine which separates off the fluids. These are pumped out of Level 7 to an earth level where they are absorbed, and the dehydrated solids are compressed and transferred to a special storage space. Logically enough—though the idea struck me with a rather chilly surprise when I heard it—this space is the space left by the food we have consumed. The planners of Level 7 could not afford to waste an inch; so the deep-freeze which contains the food also holds, on the other side of a sealed but moving wall, the sewage. As the stock of food decreases and the bulk of refuse increases, so the moving wall is pushed along by the difference in pressure and one substance takes up the space left by the other. This is a very slow process; but in 500 years what is now a filled food-storage room will have become a large sewage pit.

All this is quite interesting, but I find the idea that it will take 500 years to fill that pit rather oppressive.

MARCH 28

When I walked into the lounge today I found a trio of officers squatting on their heels in one corner of the room playing some kind of gambling game. One of them spun a coin in the air and the others were betting on whether it would fall heads or tails. They must have had quite a bit of cash in their pockets when they were brought down here, for the little piles of notes and coins in front of them were sizeable.

One of the three seemed to be enjoying the game enormously. When I first went across to watch over their shoulders he was losing, but then he had a lucky break, backing tails every time, and grew very excited. Then his luck changed once more. He started doubling up, trying to regain his losses, but in a few more spins of the coin he was cleaned out.

Anxious to stay in the game, he asked one of the other players to lend him some money. The other man asked what would happen if he lost that money too: how could he pay it back? The excited one answered that he would *not* lose. The other two grinned at each other and shrugged.

"Look," said the excited one, "my luck is bound to change soon. I've just had a bad run—all right. But it can't go on for ever. In fact it means I'll have a good run now. The law of averages, remember?"

This argument did not impress the others, and the unlucky one was still moneyless. But he could not keep quiet and with-

31

draw. Nettled by their indifference to his persuasion, he tried abuse. "You're a fool," he shouted at the man he had tried to borrow from. "Why are you so keen to hold on to your lousy money? What do you want money for down here? Can you spend it on anything? Can you buy yourself a drink? Idiot!"

This was too much for the other officer, who, being less eloquent, was on the point of assaulting the would-be borrower when the loudspeaker ordered the latter to leave the lounge immediately and await further orders in his own room. After he had left the other two players were told to do the same.

This evening an announcement came over the general loudspeaker. The incident in the lounge was mentioned, and we were told that gambling on Level 7 was strictly forbidden. It was described as an upper-earthly vice which could not be tolerated down here. It was an 'un-Level 7 activity', as the speaker put it. And she added: "There is no point in gambling here, as money has no value on Level 7." She concluded: "Money is the root of all evil! The best things in life are free!"

I was reminded of the rise in salary which my promotion had brought, and of how pleased I had been, only a week ago. Now, of course, the money meant nothing. Everything was free on Level 7. Besides, there was no room for a bank, or for a boxing ring for quarrelling gamblers. Food and sewage were infinitely more important!

MARCH 29

The idea of the sewage pit, slowly getting bigger for the next 500 years, has been on my mind for the last couple of days. I have been imagining that wall being pushed along, a fraction of an inch at a time, by accumulated foulness.

Yesterday I had the odd impression that I could smell the odours of that place. It worried me all the time, but most of all during meals. Though our food has hardly any taste at all, I thought yesterday that I had detected a distinct flavour, a nasty one. I thought to myself: 'What if the wall leaks?'

Last night the pit was with me even in my sleep. Here is what I dreamt.

I was swimming in a beautiful blue pool in a mountain region, enjoying myself immensely. I was floating on my back, looking at the sky and at the surrounding mountains with their high peaks. Then I wanted to get out, and suddenly discovered that the pool had sunk deeper and that I could not climb the slippery rocks around it. I swam from one side to another, trying to find a place where I might crawl out, but with no success. Then, imperceptibly, concrete walls replaced the mountains about me, and instead of the high blue sky I saw a grey ceiling suspended low over the pool. The clear water became dark and oily, and began to give off a disgusting stench. I swam around the pool again, looking desperately for some means of escape from the foul fluid, and found myself opposite a scale on the concrete wall. The scale was vertical, with red marks and numerals to indicate the depth of the water. As I looked at it the level of the water touched mark 127. I trod water, fixing my eyes on this number in fascination. But I could not watch it for long, because it soon disappeared beneath the water and higher numbers appeared: 137, 147, 157. . . . I realised that the water was not sinking any more, but rapidly rising. All around me were the enclosing walls, and above my head the ceiling was coming closer and closer. I could read the numbers on the scale as the water carried me relentlessly up: 327, 337, 347. And now I could see that at the very top of the scale, at the point where the wall met the ceiling, there was a sign in much bigger print: 500 YEARS. And I knew that when the water reached that point I would drown. But would it be any worse to be drowned than to be suffocated by that smell? The numbers were still rising: 457, 467, 477. . . . Then I woke up.

33

That nightmare has depressed me again. The smell, the pit, the 500 years—I cannot get them out of my head. It looks as if all my efforts to get adjusted down here have failed. I have met people, talked about things, tried to find interest in my surroundings; and all for nothing. I am back in the pit of my own depression. Just as I was during my first days here. Perhaps even worse.

It would be easier to bear all this if only I could get rid of that smell. I know it is pure imagination, because I have asked X-107 and several other people if they can smell anything, and none of them can. But still I meet it everywhere I go. I never knew one could imagine a smell so vividly. People talk about 'seeing things' and 'hearing things', but I have never come across anyone who suffered from hallucinations which made him 'smell things'. Not until now. I would gladly cut off my nose to get rid of that stench!

MARCH 31

X-107 is doing his best to get me out of my depression. He uses a peculiar method: discussing various arrangements on Level 7 and trying to find a rational explanation and a justification for each. This intellectual game sometimes becomes absorbing. Every now and then, when I am concentrating on some such riddle, I forget about the smell.

After these discussions we usually arrive at the conclusion that arrangements on Level 7 have been made in the best of all possible ways. Any alternative arrangements which we think up turn out, on examination, to be less perfect. The logical conclusion would seem to be that Level 7 is the best of all possible levels, the best of all possible worlds.

Take, for example, a simple thing such as entering the PBX Operations Room. If there were nothing to stop anybody going in there, the risk of having a pair of madmen playing with the 'typewriters' would be serious. If, instead, we four

PBX officers had special keys to the room, that too might cause trouble: somebody could steal a key, or—equally disastrous—an officer might lose it and so be prevented from entering the room quickly in case of an emergency.

To prevent all these complications, the door is opened for us when we approach it in the course of our duties, and closed to everybody else. It is quite simple: anybody walking up to the door appears on the screen of an anonymous watcher, who decides whether the person should enter the room or not and presses a button if he wants the door to open.

"But suppose," I said to X-107 today, "we conspired to push buttons at the moment when one of us was relieving the other from duty and we were both in the room. We might push them because the suspense of waiting for an order was sending us both crazy. What then? Who could prevent the two of us starting a war all on our own?"

Before X-107 could answer, the sweet voice of the loudspeaker said: "Don't worry about that! There is a supervisor on Level 7 who has to push *his* buttons, in *his* room, before PBX Operations Room is linked with the external rocket bases. So there is a safeguard against the possibility you mentioned, Officer X-127."

"You see," said X-107, "there's your answer. It's the best of all possible systems."

"And apparently," I added, "we are watched so closely that there is no chance of our going mad without the loudspeaker noticing it. Isn't that so, Miss Loudspeaker?"

The loudspeaker remained silent, and X-107 and myself promptly set about deciding what this silence meant. How should one explain it? Did it mean that the lady was no longer listening to our talk? Or was she listening but not bothering to join in?

He thought she did not listen, and I that she did not care to answer. He pointed out that she very rarely reacted to anything we said, even when she was quite capable of supplying the answer to one of our questions; which must mean that she did not listen much. I argued that when she did answer it was in response to significant questions only; so she listened a lot, but said little. Neither could prove his case. Then I remembered that I had recorded in my diary a previous instance of an answer from the loudspeaker. It might provide evidence to decide the question one way or the other. For the first time my diary might serve some practical purpose; I do not know why, but this idea pleased me immensely.

I soon found the entry—the one for March 23. I had been wondering aloud why I had been chosen for training as a push-button officer. I started reading the passage out to X-107, and I had only gone a short way, as far as the phrase 'push-button', when it seemed to me that the loudspeaker gave a little click. I stopped reading and glanced up at X-107, who grinned and nodded and pointed up at the loudspeaker to show that he had heard the sound too.

We waited in silence, but the loudspeaker said nothing.

Suddenly X-107 called out: "Push-button." There was the hardly audible click again. We waited a few moments to see if the loudspeaker would make any comment this time, and when it remained silent X-107 went on: "There you are! Behind that grille in the ceiling there must be a microphone as well as a loudspeaker. And the microphone is sensitive to a certain word—the one I said just now. The moment it's mentioned, the microphone starts working and everything we say is transmitted to the good lady, who answers if she thinks it's necessary and switches the microphone off again if she isn't interested."

"Do you think she's interested in the fact that we know how her system works now?" I said, forced to admit that X-107's hypothesis seemed correct. But I had to test it once more: "Push-button!"

No answering click was forthcoming, and I waited for X-107 to explain that one.

He chuckled. "Of course she's interested," he said. "She

hasn't switched the microphone off yet, and that's why it didn't click that time. It only clicks when it switches itself on."

"All right," I said, "you win. But if the microphone system was intended as some sort of security measure, to check that we weren't planning to push a few buttons—well, it's not much use now, is it? We can conspire away as much as we like as long as we don't mention the key phrase."

"Well," X-107 replied, "the same was true *before* we knew how the system worked, and they must have known quite well that a device sensitive to only one phrase couldn't possibly act as a guarantee against conspiracy. Personally, I don't think their intention is to spy on us in that way at all, otherwise they'd have a much more fool-proof system. They simply chose a phrase which we'd use naturally in discussing our work down here, to enable them to give a piece of advice or answer a question now and then. It's designed to help us, to see that we're not worrying about our duties."

The lady behind the system—if she was still listening— neither confirmed nor denied this, but I was convinced by X-107's argument. Certainly we PBX officers are taken very good care of down here.

And yet, the best of all possible. . . . How can one speak of *best* things in this pit of misery? While X-107 and I were arguing about the microphone today I was almost happy. But now, even while I finish writing this entry, it is coming back, that stench.

APRIL 1

Yesterday evening, and then several times this morning, we had a general warning through the loudspeaker not to play any of the tricks customary on the First of April. Level 7 cannot afford the spreading of false rumours. No April fools on Level 7.

37

The warning was, of course, a very sensible one. The arrangements in the Operations Room are so fool-proof that no one could be misled into starting an actual war; but April fooling could have very dangerous results in other ways.

Suppose somebody spread the rumour that we were going back up to the surface. Not everybody would swallow it whole; but even if they only half-believed it, it would give rise to hopes which would die a very hard death. Getting reconciled to life down here is difficult enough even if one is convinced that the chances of escape are nil.

The mere idea of getting out makes my heart beat faster. It even makes me forget the smell. One image expels the other one, just as though a fresh, earth-scented breeze from up there had really found its way down and blown away the persecuting stench.

That is all very pleasant, but thinking about that sort of thing will not do any good in the long run. The drug is too powerful. I might get to the stage where I could not prevent thoughts of escape from entering my head. I might start to believe in the possibility of getting out, and go quite mad.

No, no fooling on Level 7. This is a serious place. No tricks, no jokes, no April fools. We are all wise down here, even on April 1.

Or are we? Perhaps we are April fools all round the year. We *are* deceiving each other. We are doing it *all* the time. X-107 is deceiving me and I am deceiving him. And the soft-voiced lady on the loudspeaker is deceiving both of us. We all pretend not to feel what we do feel—and know that we feel. We are doing it all the time.

We do not deceive just other people; we deceive ourselves. Each of us is making a perpetual April fool of himself, the biggest one imaginable. Each tells himself lies which he pretends to believe, though he knows they are lies.

Quite right: no April fools on Level 7. Level 7 is the place for all-the-year-round fools.

Today I am in a better mood. I wonder why. I cannot find anything to explain it, but the fact remains that the depression I suffered yesterday and before that has lifted. I am not worried by that awful smell today. It has completely disappeared.

Perhaps the explanation is simply that I had reached the lowest point of my depression, the point where one either starts to recover or else goes completely to pieces. In my case it was recovery: I started back up from a sort of mental Level 7, and now my (still strictly mental) sky is clearing.

That reminds me: yesterday somebody explained to me how our supply of fresh air works, and that may have helped to blow the stench out of my thoughts.

I met this man, AS-127 ('AS' for Air Supply), in the lounge yesterday evening. As soon as I learnt that it was his job to provide the fresh air down here I button-holed him and got him to tell me all about it. I do not know why it seemed so important at that moment, unless I had at the back of my mind the notion that his explanation might clear my head of its imaginary bad air.

He made the whole business sound deceptively simple— though I suppose the basic principle *is* simple enough really. The problem which faced the scientists was this: how to provide a supply of clean air which was *not* drawn from the surface of the earth. To pump down air from above would have been easy, but most dangerous: it would have meant using filters to clean the air of radioactivity—unreliable things even if a bomb did not drop close enough to damage them by blast or heat.

Happily, they found a way to make us independent of air from above by imitating nature on a small scale. During the day plants on the earth turn the carbon dioxide exhaled by

39

human beings and other creatures back into oxygen. The scientists have arranged for this to happen down here too.

"It was that part," said AS-127, "the application of the principle, which was so difficult. Think of the conditions which plants normally experience: seasons, day and night, sunshine, rain, soil rich in the chemicals they need for growth —all of which simply don't exist on Level 7. So the scientists had to grow them in water with the necessary ingredients added and the temperature carefully controlled, and—most important—to provide them with artificial sunlight. Extremely complicated, but they managed it. They also found a way of growing a large number of plants in very limited space."

"But I've never seen a plant down here," I said, which made AS-127 laugh.

"I'm not surprised," he replied. "You don't suppose we grow them all round the place, do you? They're much too precious. All the plants are concentrated in one special place, and as carefully tended as the eternal flame of an old temple. Nobody may go in there except myself and the other AS officers; but you share the benefit of it through the ventilation pipes."

I could not blame him for sounding rather self-satisfied. As one of the priests in charge of the sacred air-supplying plants he had something to be proud of. His work was of vital importance *all* the time, and I must admit I felt a twinge of envy. He did not have to sit waiting, day after day, for the order which would justify his existence. But I also felt curiously reassured by what he had told me. I think it was because the system seemed, for all its technical complications, so close to nature. It is good to know that the air we breathe is not stored in jars or cleaned with chemicals.

Another thing has a soothing effect on me: music. I discovered this last night. I had turned on one of the two continuous programmes before from time to time, but only in an attack of nervous fidgets, and usually I switched it off after a few moments. Last night, however, X-107 spent a long time listening to the classical tape, under the impression that I was asleep. I lay awake with my eyes closed, letting the sound flow around me, and by and by I drifted into a state of utter tranquillity in which all my senses except hearing died away and I was aware of nothing but the music. This morning I listened to the music again, to see if the experience would repeat itself, and, sure enough, it did.

Perhaps the effect is like that of a narcotic. But the drug is not a dangerous one, like dreaming about going up to the surface. Music is a sedative without after-effects—as far as I can tell at the moment, anyway. I shall try to make good use of it from now on, whenever it is needed.

One more good thing about this drug is that it does not run short. The addict can take a dose whenever he feels like it by simply switching on the everlasting programme. It *does* seem to be lasting for ever, too. People who have been listening persistently since the first day say that so far not a single tune has been repeated. I wonder how long those tapes are.

APRIL 3

This is really funny. Yesterday I wondered how long the music tapes were. Today, at dinner, a rumour was going round that the tunes of the first day were being repeated. Some music fans swore they heard Beethoven's 'Eroica' on March 21, and yesterday they heard it again. Listeners to the programme of light music were saying the same thing, though I forget what tunes they said had come round for the second time.

So the music tapes are twelve days long. This is pretty long, one must admit, but still it is disappointing. At dinner everybody seemed a little saddened by the discovery, not only the music fans. It made me sad too. I wonder why.

I have never been a great music-lover. There are a couple

41

of dozen classical pieces I enjoy listening to, certainly; but I have never had much interest in new stuff—either really new music, or just new to me. What I had heard of the selection on the tape was quite to my taste, and as far as I was concerned the amount of music on a twelve-day tape was plenty.

And yet the discovery that the tape was only twelve days long did give me a sharp pang of regret. And it would not have made any difference if the time had been longer: if the tape had run for a month, or a year, and then somebody had told me that it had just started at the beginning again, it would have given me the same sensation. It was the fact that the tape was *limited* that saddened me.

I wanted something, just something, on Level 7 to be unlimited. I suppose it is only human to crave things which are not limited as humans are. Perhaps this is one reason why people—up there—enjoy breathing fresh air: there is such an inexhaustible lot of it. For the same reason they like looking out over the ocean, which they know goes on beyond the visible horizon; or travelling across the water to places they have never seen before; or standing where they are and looking up at the night sky.

To us on Level 7—I think this was everybody's sensation today—the seemingly unending stream of music held the last surviving suggestion of boundlessness, of infinity. Everything else was calculated and cut down to suit our needs. Space was limited, and the smallness of the rooms emphasised the limitations of our existence. The meals were the very opposite of infinite in their variety. The company was limited. Even the atomic energy supply was limited: enough for a thousand years it might be, but still we knew it had a limit.

Only the tape seemed to have no ending. It was the sea and the sky. It was the green jungle waiting for our exploring feet. Though our common sense told us this was ridiculous, it was immortality.

It was the tape of life—real life, not cave-existence. It added some colour to our grey days, and shone into the gloom of our

42

despair as if a sunbeam from up there had broken all the rules and strayed down into Level 7.

But it appears that the tape is only twelve days long.

No doubt about it now: both music tapes are twelve days long. They are repeating themselves, and if we feel inclined we can start to make exact schedules of what we shall be hearing in twelve days, a fortnight, a month, or ten years. All we have to do is to mark each day on a calendar what tune is played at what hour, and then mark the same tune at the same time twelve days ahead and twenty-four days ahead and thirty-six days and so on as long as the calendar lasts. What a horrible idea.

Nobody has started to make schedules yet, as far as I know. But people have been talking about the tapes a great deal for the last twenty-four hours. Even X-107 has been a bit depressed by this business. He does not say so, but I can sense it. He seems to have lost his enthusiasm for the music, and if I switch on the tape he asks me if I would mind turning it off. The music must have meant more to him than to me.

Even so, I cannot get him to admit that he resents the limited supply of music. To him Level 7 is still the best of all possible worlds. When I suggested that they could at least have arranged for a tape that would run for a man's lifetime, so that he might never know when it came to an end and started again, X-107 retorted that this was absurd.

"Level 7," he said, "is limited, *very* limited, in space. You can see that for yourself. There's no room for luxuries. Think of the difficulty of providing the basic necessities for five hundred people to live down here for half a millennium: enough food, supplies and energy to make us a completely self-sufficient community over four thousand feet underground —when until recently sub-continents found it hard enough

43

to be self-sufficient on the *surface* of the globe. To achieve all this is nothing less than a miracle of human ingenuity and scientific progress."

"You make me feel grateful," I remarked sarcastically, "that we have recorded music at all."

"And so you should," replied X-107. "They made room down here for a lounge. You don't expect a concert hall as well, do you?"

"All right, but what about books?" I said. "Sometimes I wish I had something to read besides my own diary. I suppose you'll say I should be grateful for the paper I write on."

"Would you rather starve in a library?"

At that I gave up the argument. It was clear that X-107 would never be convinced by my point of view, because he would never allow himself to be convinced: it was necessary for him to believe in the inevitability of the arrangements on Level 7, because only in that way could he console himself for their disadvantages.

So because there is limited space on Level 7 there is no room for a very long music-tape; and if there is no room for a long tape there is no room for the idea of infinity. Better forget it.

APRIL 5

While I had a shower today I was thinking of the problem of space on Level 7, and it struck me how odd it was that the planners should think it necessary to give X-107 and me a bathroom to ourselves. Surely all four PBX officers could have shared one bathroom. If it came to that, ten men could use the same bathroom without getting in each other's way much.

Half an hour later I met P-867 in the lounge again, and as usual she cornered me and started talking. By an odd coincidence—or maybe it was because I looked fresh and smelled of soap—she complained that she could not take a shower today. I asked her why not, and she explained that they had only one shower per fifty women. Each of them could take a shower once in two and a half days at a fixed hour, and missing one's hour meant going without for another two and a half days. And she had missed her turn last time. Even the toilet, she mentioned incidentally, had to be shared by twenty women.

This was very strange, I said, and pointed out to her (not without feeling rather superior) that we PBX officers had one bathroom between two. I was more surprised than ever at the degree of comfort we enjoyed.

Not so P-867, who had a ready explanation for it all. "The type of man selected for PBX operations," she said, "would have a compulsion to clean himself frequently. For men like you and your fellow-officers, to be deprived of the comfort of a well-equipped and ever-available bathroom would not be just an inconvenience, but a serious disturbance. You might develop neurotic symptoms and goodness knows what else! So it's perfectly reasonable the way it is."

It occurred to me that I did like to wash my hands often, though I had never thought of it in terms of psychological compulsion. It seemed simply a hygienic habit. Still, her explanation made me feel rather uneasy—as her remarks usually did—and to hide my confusion I said something about the principle of equality and about chivalry towards women. On both these grounds one could argue that P-867 and the others were entitled to as much comfort as we PBX officers enjoyed.

She said this was absolute nonsense. "That old prejudice, chivalry, is completely out of date in an atomic era," she asserted, adding with a laugh: "Next thing, you'll want to fight rockets on horseback and wearing armour." And as for equality, this was a principle which had no place on Level 7. I was doing a different job from hers, and I had been selected for this job because I myself was different in my emotional set-up. The facilities which I enjoyed were not a privilege,

45

but were necessary if I was to do my job efficiently, and that was all there was to it.

"But what about *your* job?" I asked. "Doesn't your comfort make any difference?"

"Not as much," she answered. "Take this washing business: a psychologist would get rid of that compulsion in himself— if he ever had it—long before he finished his training. I find our overcrowded bathroom a nuisance, of course, but it wouldn't make me neurotic even if I couldn't wash for a month." And she giggled.

That remark struck me as most unpleasant, and for a moment I could not help feeling physically repelled by her. It occurred to me that if she were a *perfect* mistress of her science she would have been more wary of telling me about her disregard for hygiene—if she cared what I thought of her, as she seemed to.

APRIL 6

Earlier today the loudspeaker announced that a new programme will be inaugurated on Level 7: a series of live talks entitled 'Know Thy Level'. The half-hour talks, to be given daily, will cover various aspects of life on Level 7.

This announcement has aroused a fair amount of interest. People down here have begun to look around them and learn about their environment, if only in a despairing attempt to adjust themselves to something they instinctively dislike. The new talks will be instructive, besides relieving the monotony.

People are especially curious about the fact that these will be *live* talks and not tape-recorded ones. There is such a lot of automation down here that one comes to assume that anything like a series of talks will have been canned long in advance, to be served up when and as often as required. That this is not the case is some consolation for the twelve-day limit of the music tapes, if one can judge by the fact that some of

46

the people who took that business hardest have been discussing the new programme most enthusiastically. X-107 thinks the talks will be very interesting: "We've got to know the world we live in, haven't we?" he remarked just now.

I wonder if this programme may not have been specially arranged to counteract the disappointment felt over the music tapes. It is in their interest not to let us get too depressed.

Perhaps not. It could equally as well be that the programme was planned from the start, but not put out until we had had time to get adjusted to the new conditions. In the first few days down here most people would have been brooding too much to pay any attention to a series of lectures; but now that the initial shock has passed the talks may consolidate whatever adjustment we have been able to make.

It must be X-107's influence which makes me puzzle about it like this. Through my discussions with him I seem to have acquired his habit of analysing every event and arrangement and weighing various arguments and alternatives. To begin with I took one side and X-107 took another, but these days it seems that I can do without him: I carry on the dialogues with myself, inventing arguments both for and against any given theory. I suppose this must mean that I am becoming more self-sufficient. A self-sufficient citizen of the self-sufficient world of Level 7.

Anyway, we shall soon learn all about the arrangements on Level 7. We shall understand the instructions which at present we just blindly carry out. So far we have been given commands—dehydrated mental food; now we shall be given the reasons for the commands—a real juicy meal. At least, I hope so.

The first programme is due any time now, and I shall have to break off writing this to listen to it. Here comes the announcement: the first talk in the new 'Know Thy Level' series, 'Communications on Level 7'.

The talk is over. It was delivered in a clear and lively man-

47

ner—by a woman, but not one of those who usually make announcements through the loudspeaker. A rather deep contralto voice. I would like to hear her sing.

The talk itself contained little that I did not know before. It explained the elaborate communications system on Level 7.

There was first the 'general' loudspeaker system whose announcements were heard everywhere—in working-rooms, in private rooms, in the lounge, in bathrooms and so on. Then there was the 'functional' system which transmitted instructions to a specific branch of the crew—the psychologists, say, or the PBX officers. Lastly there was the 'private' system which occasionally reacted to the problems of individual men and women. The three systems worked interdependently over the same set of speakers, and if it happened that two or more systems were competing for the use of the loudspeaker at the same time, the one which had priority would automatically cut out the others. In order of priority the functional system always came first, the general second and the private last.

The crew had means of communicating with the command as well. One had only to press one of the special red buttons (evidently connected to microphones) and one's voice would be received by the communications centre and there, as at a telephone exchange, be connected to the appropriate authority, according to the nature of the message. But this system was to be used only in cases of real emergency: sickness, malfunctioning of installations, and things like that. (The speaker made no mention of hidden microphones operating without the button, such as the one X-107 and I detected in our room the other day. Perhaps they are only installed in PBX officers' rooms.)

I had noticed the red buttons around before, of course, with their instructions: "In case of emergency press and speak." But I have never used one so far. The only times I have felt like doing so were when I wanted to shout: "Let me out of here."

The talk was restricted to Level 7's internal communications. There was no mention of contact between Level 7 and the outside world, though this must exist or we should never know when to push the buttons or anything else. Information on *that* topic would have been fascinating, because it would have been a link with all we had left behind up there. Which is probably why it was not included in the talk: they do not want anything to remind us of life on the surface; we must get adjusted to life 4,400 feet down. So, no talk of any world outside *our* world.

This gives an ironical twist to 'Know Thy Level'. "Don't bother about other worlds," the title seems to say. "Know about the only one you'll ever live in."

APRIL 7

An extraordinary thing happened in the lounge today. Usually people there form small groups of two or three, talking quietly with each other, and often hardly speaking at all. This time the picture was different. One man—I was told later that he was a philosopher, Ph-107—was standing and talking, vigorously and persuasively, while all the rest listened in silence, sitting or standing around.

The scene was most unusual. Not only had I never observed it on Level 7 before, but I do not remember coming across informal public speech-making like this up above either. It was like a return to the old oratory. In ancient city-states people must have talked, and listened, in that way.

Strange as it may seem, the subject of the man's speech was Democracy—Democracy on Level 7, to be precise.

The topic seemed to fascinate his audience. Even P-867, who likes talking herself, was absorbed and hardly noticed me. Other people drifted into the room from time to time while the philosopher was speaking, and all their conversations died as they were drawn into the rapt circle of listeners.

Ph-107's thesis went something like this.

49

Democracy, he said, is the rule of all over all. To make it practicable, however, men have always found it necessary to compromise: to follow the decisions of the majority. And as the actual ruling power must perforce be in the hands of a very few people chosen as the representatives of the majority, it has been possible for some cynics to maintain that real democracy can never work. It is always an *élite* which rules.

To forestall such objections, people have tried to limit the power of the *élite* by devising impersonal machinery of government such as laws, constitutions, principles. The rule of law, as opposed to the rule of people, has been the basis of democracy from time immemorial.

All right, the cynic will reply, but the rule of laws and constitutions and so forth remains, ultimately, the rule of *some* people—the people who devised them, in this or past ages. Principles cannot invent themselves. And when all the rules have been laid down they still have to be applied and interpreted by lawyers, judges, politicians—by people.

These objections, said Ph-107, cannot be disregarded. They have formed a valid criticism of every form of democracy which has existed—until today. Now, for the first time in the history of mankind, perfect, absolute democracy is coming into being: democracy on Level 7.

As we gathered yesterday from the talk about communications, there is no personal authority here. One does not have to salute anybody. "We obey only *impersonal* commands," Ph-107 cried with enthusiasm, thumping one fist into the palm of his other hand. "We acknowledge only the authority of the loudspeaker—the impersonal, the supra-personal personification of all of us.

"This is," he wound up, "the ultimate logical form for democracy to take: purged of personal elements, refined until the quintessence, the very abstraction, is all that remains. Democracy on Level 7 is the only true democracy, not only in the world today, but in the whole of human history."

For a few moments after he had finished there was si-

50

lence among us. Then a man at the back objected, diffidently: "Surely somebody must be sitting at the other end of the loudspeaker and giving the orders?"

Ph-107's answer was startling: "What proof have you of that? Perhaps it's only a tape! And even if it's a living person it doesn't matter, for he's completely anonymous and so represents us all. Think of folk art and folk songs: at some time somebody must have created them, but their anonymity makes them both the expression and the possession of the people."

At this he smiled triumphantly, and then added: "Any more questions?"

It seemed that somebody—it was a woman this time—was not altogether happy about his reasoning. "Do you imply," she asked, "that the rule of the loudspeaker, just because it's impersonal, must therefore be the rule of the majority and not of an *élite?*"

"Not merely of the majority," came the philosopher's ready reply. "It is the rule of *all*. Don't we all, implicitly or explicitly, agree with each command we receive? Isn't each order the most sensible one which could be given, in the present circumstances? Anyone can, if he tries, find the good reason behind every instruction. And when you've discovered the reason, you must agree that the loudspeaker has given the very order which you yourself would have given if the decision had been yours." He smiled sweetly at the woman who had asked the question, and then around at his circle of listeners. "Is there anybody here who can give me one single example of a command with which he or she disagrees?"

"The command to go down to Level 7," I felt like saying. But I realised that this order was given before we got here, and so did not qualify—not that the argument would have served any useful purpose anyway.

So, 'in the present circumstances', I said nothing.

The speaker seemed to have carried his point, for nobody had any more objections or questions for him to answer before the loudspeaker announced that our time in the lounge was up; whereupon, of our own free will, and therefore democratically, we left. Ph-107 alone stayed behind in the room —apparently to repeat his speech to the next lot of people. I thought that, in the present circumstances, this would be most salutary. And of course the loudspeaker must have agreed with me and given the appropriate instructions to Ph-107.

APRIL 9

I have been busier than usual for the last few days—longer on duty, because X-117 is sick. I do not know what is the matter with him. His room-mate says it is something 'psychological'. And I find my spare time passes more quickly too— talking, arguing about things with X-107, listening to the 'Know Thy Level' talks.

The talks are disappointingly boring, though. Today we were given a thorough explanation of our diet. I did not listen at all attentively—a talk about a tasteless diet does not make the meals any more appetising.

One thing I did learn from this talk was that our food takes the form it does, not only because of the lack of space for storage, but also to suit the peculiar living conditions of Level 7. It contains all the necessary calories, vitamins, minerals and so forth. It is unflavoured in order to prevent excessive appetite, which would be undesirable: people would want more than their carefully calculated ration; and, if they got it, they would put on weight, and then their health would suffer because of the lack of opportunities for exercise. Due consideration has been given to the problems of digestion, the prevention of stomach troubles, and so on—I think the pills we get at lunch-time have something to do with it. Back on the surface I never suffered from stomach trouble, but even so I must confess I was surprised how easily my stomach took to the new food (or lack of food) down here.

I suppose all this information was not self-evident, and that the nutrition experts have done a splendid job of work. But the talk about it was boring.

Yesterday's talk was even more tedious, in fact I cannot even remember what it was about. No doubt it too contrived to suggest that we were living in the best of all possible ways.

Complete self-sufficiency, thanks to our wonderful scientists—and all enjoyed under perfect democracy, according to Ph-107. What could be better?

But no sunshine.

I wonder what put that into my head again. It is a pity there is no ingredient in the food to make me forget it. Even the science of nutrition seems to have its limits.

APRIL 10

In the lounge today P-867 mentioned that her fellow-psychologist was treating a very interesting case. "It's a certain officer who has a very important function," she said, obviously hoping to intrigue me and get me talking. "Though, of course," she added with an arch smile, "everybody has a vital job on Level 7."

As it happened, her remark *did* interest me, because it sounded as if the patient might be the sick PBX officer. I described him and she confirmed that this was indeed the man.

I cannot say I had got to know X-117 at all well. When he was off duty he kept mostly to the room he shares with X-137, opposite ours, and I had hardly exchanged more than a few words with him before he went sick. But what made his case interesting for me was not his personality but his function. He had been doing exactly the same job as myself, and so besides feeling a mild *esprit de corps* inspired by the illness of my fellow button-pusher I was curious to know just what had happened to him. I was also wondering how serious his illness was, because while he is away I am on duty for eight instead of six hours each day.

P-867 saw that she had aroused my interest, and started supplying information at once.

The trouble with X-117, she maintained, was that he was a bad choice for Level 7. He really should not have been here at all. One of the essential conditions of selection for work down here, irrespective of what form the work would take, was that the candidate should have no strong personal attachment to anybody remaining on earth. For that reason the selectors excluded not only married persons, but also anybody who was at all close to parents, children or friends of either sex. "It's one more way of making sure that people down here are psychologically self-sufficient," she said.

My own recollections bear out what she said. I remember being asked at great length, during one of the interviews prior to my selection for PBX training, what family and friends I had, and what were my feelings towards them. At the time I assumed that the questions were aimed at seeing whether I was safe from the security angle. Fortunately (though I would have said *un*fortunately if I had known what the questions really meant) I had no strong family ties and no intimate friendships.

P-867 told me that she too was a self-sufficient person—what some laymen would call a lonely person—and so she too was considered suitable for Level 7. According to her, however, the selectors did not depend entirely on direct information about social relationships. The facts supplied by the person being interviewed were supplemented by indirect psychological evidence. The candidate told the selectors about his past and present relationships. But by various questions which were included in the long psychological tests (concerning the purpose of which the candidate knew nothing) the interviewers also found out about his propensity to form relationships in the future. The training would have been wasted if

54

they had chosen a person who happened to be unattached but was basically sociable, for he might have formed some close attachment while he was a trainee and so made himself quite unsuitable for transference to Level 7.

In spite of the care taken over these tests, they seem to have slipped up over X-117. According to P-867, the man is not psychologically self-sufficient. True, he severed all contact with his parents as a boy and became independent at the age of fifteen—there was some long-standing family discord which made him leave home as soon as he could. In every other respect too he seemed just the man for Level 7. But now he is showing symptoms of an attachment to his mother!

"In terms of psychology this is quite a simple case," P-867 assured me. "A neurotic regression to childhood brought on by the stress of new conditions. But," she added, "the psychologist who tested him up there should never have made such a terrible mistake. It was his job to weed out people like that and to find types immune to such neurotic tendencies. We just can't afford to have sociable people on Level 7." (Smirk and giggle.)

The time was up and I was happy to leave the lounge. I felt sorry for X-117, but at the same time I envied him. There he was, suffering, perhaps going off his head—but on account of an emotional attachment to his mother, to another human being. I might miss the sunshine and spend hours brooding about that, but I never lost sleep over a *person* up there. I suddenly realised how much poorer I was than my fellow-officer in his misery. I, along with P-867 and probably everybody else on Level 7, was psychologically self-sufficient. My well-being depended hardly at all on the presence of anyone else. Most likely I was incapable of love; and so was everyone else here, except for X-117. And *therefore* I was just the person to live here.

Now I feel sorry for myself. I am sitting here alone at the desk and probably do not need—not much, at least—any company. But I wish I did. Why can I not care more for other people?—people up there or people down here, it does not matter which. It is as if my soul were deformed, or part of it has been amputated.

I suppose it is just as well I was made the way I am. If we all felt the way X-117 feels, this place would by now be one great lunatic asylum, all patients and no attendants. Level 7 could not possibly fulfil its function, it could not exist. It is obviously best as it is.

But I wish I could pity X-117 more than I do.

APRIL 11

Am I capable, or am I not capable, of pitying other people? Am I, or am I not, able to develop a genuine friendship, to love somebody, to care for another person with all my heart?

This business has been plaguing me since yesterday. I do not want to be a monster, and a man without emotions *is* a monster. What is the difference between me and an electronic brain? It can calculate far better, work more efficiently; it makes no mistakes. It cannot get fond of anybody. Neither can I.

But I can pity myself and torment myself, and an electronic gadget cannot do that. *There's* the difference.

Level 7. The unsocial society. Community of self-pitying gadgets, hive of monsters.

Are we really monsters, or merely miserable creatures who deserve pity? There I go—self-pity again! But I did say 'are *we*', which may be evidence of sociability in me after all.

How deep does it go? Oh, I wish I could stop fretting about it. If I were a real machine I should be much happier.

A happy gadget! I had better stop writing for today and listen to some music, if all I can produce is such absolute nonsense. Perhaps I am heading for a nervous breakdown myself.

Something for the psychologists to think about: Can a man

become neurotic through worrying about his inability to be neurotic?

I am not finding the 'Know Thy Level' talks as interesting as I thought I would. Today they tried to explain the system of personal identification on Level 7. Everybody's 'name' ends with the digit 7, because we live on Level 7. The letters at the beginning refer to functions, which everybody knew anyway; and the other two figures have some more complicated explanation which I did not try to understand. No doubt there is a system behind it, as with everything else down here.

When the talk was over X-107 tried to discuss with me the reason for our calling each other by letters and numbers instead of personal or family names—a practice which we were persuaded to adopt back at the training camp, so it comes quite naturally on Level 7. The reason behind it, he thought, was that the old names would have nostalgic associations with life on the surface and so would make it harder for us to get adjusted to our new existence.

It may well be so, but I was not interested in discussing it. What did interest me was X-107's efforts to make me talk in spite of my evident lack of enthusiasm, because he realised I was upset about something; as he had done on previous occasions. Which must mean that he felt some concern about me. And if he is not entirely unsociable, then perhaps my own case is not so hopeless either.

My speculations engaged me so, I hardly listened to what he was saying. Suppose we were not entirely unsociable, I thought, only less sociable than most people—people up there. Suppose the difference were of this sort—one of degree, not of kind—well, the implications would be enormous. I might at least be capable of *liking* somebody.

57

As the saying goes: 'If the fire doesn't boil the kettle, it may stop it freezing.' Perhaps X-117 is not the only sociable fish to slip through the psychologists' net.

APRIL 14

I see that my last entry ended with a slightly envious reference to X-117. But it seems that his sociable tendencies are bringing him nothing but more trouble. P-867 is now participating in his therapy, and she told me today that his condition is getting more serious. He cannot move the fingers of his right hand.

She says there is nothing physically wrong with the hand: the paralysis is a clear symptom of hysteria. And she has a theory to explain it. At least, she has the modesty to *call* it a theory. Knowing her, I am sure she thinks it is the only possible explanation.

My fellow-officer, she says, must as a child have used his right hand in quest of pleasures which were strictly forbidden by his parents. Those urges became repressed, but they remained a powerful factor in his unconscious mind. The repressive control will not let them out even now, so the urges express themselves through the symptoms of paralysis. X-117 really enjoys his paralysis, according to P-867's strange explanation, because it is unconsciously associated with the repressed urges. But these symptoms are so remote from their true origin that the repressive control cannot recognise them and so lets them be.

In fact, X-117 has his own, seemingly 'rational' explanation for his sickness. What he says is that his paralysis is a punishment from 'above' for his readiness to push buttons and destroy the world. He keeps talking about this punishment, which he considers just. "Obviously," said P-867 today, "he doesn't *want* to be cured. His job on Level 7, pushing buttons,

58

is too strongly associated in his mind with the activities which his parents told him were wicked."

I asked her whether, on the other hand, there was not a part of his mind which *did* want to be cured: if pushing the buttons was associated with sensations of pleasure, would he not want to be capable of indulging in it? "You forget," she answered with a smile of superior wisdom, "that the repressive controls wouldn't allow it. Only under the disguise of paralysis can he have his gratification."

As if this were not enough, there appeared to be further complications. On the level of his conscious mind, X-117 resents pushing the buttons not only because it would cause general destruction but also because it would be a crime against his mother in particular. "If it were against his father," P-867 argued, "this would be a more straightforward case of Oedipus complex. But by substituting his mother for his father he complicates the issue and creates a more profound conflict, for he's very strongly attached to his mother —abnormally so, by the standards of Level 7 psychology. This is what makes him refuse so stubbornly to do anything against her. His reluctance wouldn't be nearly so great if he imagined he was going to destroy his father."

I must say I got pretty muddled by all this. Now I do not know whether X-117 is suffering from paralysis because he enjoys it, or because he does not want to push the buttons, or because he believes in God and thinks there is a divine edict against button-pushing, or because he has mixed up his parents. Probably I have mixed up P-867's explanations just as badly.

I do not really care what is the true reason for his paralysis. What affects me is the fact that he is strongly attached (to a degree considered abnormal in this abnormal place) to another human being. The idea fascinates me. To care that much must be a wonderful sensation. When I first heard

59

about X-117's paralysis I felt glad it was his hand and not mine. Now I envy him his abnormality.

APRIL 15

Our resident philosopher, Ph-107, held forth in the lounge again today. His subject was 'Freedom on Level 7'.

This time his audience was less attentive, and one or two people broke away to talk quietly among themselves in a corner. The rest listened with half an ear. Perhaps they could not think of anything better to do.

Ph-107 was saying that on Level 7 we enjoyed not only perfect democracy but also absolute freedom. When we were not on duty we could do whatever we liked. Most important, we could discuss quite freely the arrangements on Level 7. There was no secrecy, everything having been planned for the good of all and nothing needing to be hidden from our understanding.

"It is this, really, which gives our life down here the perfection which it could not achieve up above," he said. "Back there precautions had to be taken against subversion, against enemy spies, against misunderstanding. All that meant curtailing the freedom of the individual for the benefit of society. Here, on Level 7, there are no such dangers. We are hermetically cut off from enemy and ally alike, from spies and from over-inquisitive friends, from strangers and from the ignorant masses. Here everybody is known and everybody is knowing. Everybody can enjoy the individuality which his personal number symbolises. Nobody has contact with the spiritually inferior, though materially superior, outer world—indeed, it is *because* we are materially cut off from the world that we are able to develop the spiritual side of our natures to this extent. This is true freedom, a freedom which only Level 7 can give."

He went on in this style, trying to show that liberty could

not be misused here, for people chosen to live on Level 7 were reasonable, had little individual power (being dependent on all their fellows), and so on and so forth.

I had some questions I felt like asking—notably, whether a man condemned to solitary confinement but allowed to hammer his head against the wall of his cell could be called free—but I decided to say nothing. What was the use? Let him hammer his speech against us and imagine that he is free. If he believes in what he says, that is.

I was too bored to listen to his speech right to the end, and left the lounge before our time was up. I thought I would rather lie down here on my bunk and listen to some music.

APRIL 16

Today a sensational announcement, addressed to all the crew of Level 7, was repeated several times over the general loudspeaker system. As nearly as I can remember it, the wording was as follows:

"Attention, please, attention everybody! This message is for all members of the crew of Level 7. It is announced that arrangements have been made for marriages on Level 7. If you want to get married, and if the person you wish to marry accepts your proposal, all you have to do is press one of the red buttons, identify yourself, and say: 'I intend to marry So-and-so'. You will subsequently be told, through your private loudspeaker, where and when the marriage will take place.

"If you would like to marry somebody but do not feel, for any reason, like proposing directly, or if you have no opportunity to do so, you may make use of the marriage mediation service. You simply have to press the red button, identify yourself, and say: 'I should like to marry So-and-so. Please mediate.' Your proposal will be transmitted to the appropriate person, and you will receive his or her answer by private loudspeaker.

61

"You may send either sort of message at any time around the clock, for it will be automatically tape-recorded before being transferred to the appropriate section. Thank you."

This repeated announcement was followed up this evening by a short 'special' talk in the 'Know Thy Level' series. The speaker explained the great significance of marriage as a social institution from time immemorial. Then came a eulogy on the psychological benefits enjoyed by married couples. Finally—and this was the climax of her argument for marriage—she reminded us of our duty (our 'obligation to humanity', she called it) to carry on the existence of the human race in the safe living-conditions of Level 7.

While these stirring thoughts were sinking in she added a few practical details. The number of men on Level 7 was exactly the same as the number of women—250 of each; everybody therefore stood a fair chance of finding a partner. Marriages had been taken into consideration when Level 7 was planned. All the men and women were very healthy and stood the best possible chance of having healthy offspring. Moreover, as their ages were all between twenty and thirty, their children would reach adulthood in time to take over the running of Level 7.

"Necessarily, it will not be possible for married couples to have their own living-quarters," the speaker went on. "The lack of space, as well as the performance of duties, requires the continuation of the present system of living-rooms attached to working-rooms. However, special rooms for married couples have been provided, and will be allotted to each couple for a certain period each day. There are ten such rooms, which means that if everybody is married there will be approximately one hour of privacy for each couple every day."

The speaker ended by wishing all prospective couples good luck. "Don't be shy," she said. "Choose your mate and push the nearest red button."

The announcement about marriage facilities has created quite a stir on Level 7. At meals, when about a third of the crew meets at one time along the long table (we eat in three shifts), people do not take the nearest place on the bench as they used to, but wander around trying to find an attractive partner of the opposite sex. This results in some disorder, but 'promotes the interests of humanity'.

Nobody seems to be in love, as far as I can tell: probably we are incapable of feeling a strong social emotion like that, with the exception of X-117 and perhaps some other people who have come here by mistake. But at least things are a bit livelier than they were. Somebody who did not know what it was all about might think we had just enjoyed a glass of brandy. If this keeps up, it will not be long before the 500 bachelors and spinsters on Level 7 have become 250 married couples.

This evening I discussed the marriage business with X-107. He thought it all quite reasonable. I asked where space could be found for the new generations to live. He replied that if ten rooms had been set aside in advance for the convenience of married couples, space for children must have been thought of as well. This argument seemed sound enough to me.

"Of course," he added, "they must have fixed on an optimum number of people for Level 7, and if too many children are born then birth control will have to be introduced. But this problem isn't likely to arise for two or three years."

Today the loudspeaker announced the engagement of TN-237 to AS-167, one of the air-supply officers. 'TN' stands for

Teacher and Nurse—a new designation, somebody told me: previously she was known as R-237, 'R' meaning Reserve. This reserve of officers will eventually fill a variety of posts.

I do not know AS-167, but when his fiancée was pointed out to me at lunch today I recognised her as one of the women who regularly eat on my meal shift. She was congratulated by everybody sitting near her, myself included. She is a girl of about twenty, she looks nice, and today—though I would not say she was as radiant as a young bride could be—she certainly seemed more satisfied than the people around her.

The marriage ceremony, being the first one on Level 7, was broadcast over the general loudspeaker system. It was scheduled for '7 p.m.'. Perhaps this time was chosen—and announced thus, instead of in the more usual form of 19.00 hours —to make a symbolic link between the ceremony and Level 7.

I was taking a shower when 7 p.m. came round, but the noise of the water did not prevent my hearing the loudspeaker in the bathroom. Sharp at the appointed hour, it announced: "Attention, please, attention! Here is an event which makes history: the first marriage on Level 7. Everybody on Level 7 is privileged to share in this historic experience."

This announcement struck me as unusually pompous; in the normal way the loudspeaker's tone is laconic and dry. What followed, however, was as simple a marriage ceremony as could be imagined.

A woman's voice sounded: "Do you, AS-167, want to marry TN-237 and to maintain this status as long as it is mutually agreeable?"

A man's voice replied: "Yes, I do."

Then the mistress-of-ceremonies asked TN-237 a similar question, and on getting the same answer announced: "AS-167 and TN-237 are now a married couple. The names of both will from now on carry the suffix small 'm'. Congratulations!"

The whole business could not have lasted a minute, and I

was still towelling myself in the bathroom when the loud-speaker announced that the ceremony was over, and for some reason congratulated TN-237m and AS-167m again—stressing the 'm'. Perhaps these extra congratulations were due to their being the first couple to marry on Level 7. I believe the loud-speaker did mention the fact.

I put on some clothes, switched on the classical music tape and lay down on my bed. The concluding chords of Chopin's 'Funeral March' died away in the small room.

'Well,' I thought, 'if I had been the planner of Level 7 I would have arranged for Mendelssohn's "Wedding March" or some other suitable tune to be played at that juncture. If most marriages were to be performed at 7 p.m., this could easily have been co-ordinated with the twelve-day tape.

'So the arrangements on Level 7 are *not* perfect, after all!' flashed through my mind, and the notion rather pleased me.

APRIL 20

At lunch today TN-237m—the additional symbol was at-tached to her identity badge—told us some details about the marriage ceremony.

It was performed (to the visible disappointment of some of the people, mostly women, who were listening to her) in the little room where we take our laundry, a tiny closet-like place about five feet square. Only she and AS-167 were present, but evidently they must have been on the screen of the mistress-of-ceremonies, for they were told over a loudspeaker not to face each other, as they initially did, but to face the wall op-posite the door. Presumably this enabled the loudspeaker-lady to see them better.

Then they were asked the questions and gave the answers which we all heard over the general loudspeaker system, and as the mistress-of-ceremonies was congratulating them two little letters 'm' rattled down the chute which returns the

65

bundles of clean laundry. On the back each read: "Fix this to your identity badge". (TN-237m turned hers round, and we all read the instruction on the back.)

"And that was all," she concluded, looking as disappointed as any of us.

Somebody murmured that this all sounded very interesting, but he said it in such a way that it was clear he did not believe his own words. Then someone else remarked that the marriage ceremony was only a symbol: the essence of marriage, he said, lay in its essence.

Nobody contradicted this statement and the topic was dropped as the band on the table started moving and our meal glided to a stop before us. We ate without saying much until, just as we were on the point of concluding our lunch with three pills and a drink, somebody had the good or the bad idea of taking one of the pills between his thumb and forefinger and lifting it the way a glass of wine is lifted for a toast. "To TN-237m," he proposed, bowing slightly to her, "and may she enjoy many happy years with AS-167m."

"TN-237m," we all mumbled, solemnly raising our pills before popping them into our mouths; and she, deciding that our gesture was well-meaning, looked a little bashful and replied: "Thank you."

APRIL 21

A few more marriage announcements were made today. One of the wastage officers, W-297, has married a female administrator, Ad-327. R-287, male, has married a loudspeaker officer, L-267. M-227, a medical doctor, is now the wife of one of the screen-watchers, Sc-167.

Today in the lounge I tried to chat with the nurse I met on my first visit to that room, N-527. I have had little chance to speak to her since that occasion, because E-647, the electrical engineer, has always been around her, while P-867 is always around me. Today, by a happy coincidence, E-647 was missing as well as P-867, who has not shown up in the lounge for the last three days.

N-527 is rather nice. If I marry down here at all, I should like to marry her.

I asked her how her job differed from that of TN-237m, Level 7's first bride. She said that she was trained to nurse adults, while 'TN' indicated a person qualified as kindergarten teacher and nurse for babies and young children.

Then I asked her if she was kept busy. She said no, for there were very few accidents down here, and hardly any sickness so far. I suggested that this might make her life boring. She replied that she spent a lot of time listening to music—to the light tape, not the classical.

Wouldn't marriage be an additional distraction? I suggested. She answered that she did not feel a need for any additional distraction. "Still, I may marry," she said. "E-647 proposed to me yesterday, and I promised to give him an answer today, but he hasn't come." She looked around the room with a slight air of disappointment.

I did not ask her what her answer would be, but changed the subject. Though I liked her calm, hardly sensitive nature, I did not feel too cut up about the prospect of her marrying E-647. Apparently he cared for her more than I did.

Perhaps E-647 is less unsociable than I.

APRIL 22

P-867 reappeared in the lounge today. She was in even better spirits than usual, and came straight up to me. "What do you think about the marriages?" she said. "Aren't they wonderful?"

I made some cynical remark to the effect that marriage was an affliction as old as humanity itself. She laughed it off and said: "Oh, I know you don't mean that! You're only talking like that in an attempt to hide your real feelings." At this she giggled in her typical way.

I did not argue the point, but asked her where she had been the last few days.

"You missed me, didn't you?" she said with satisfaction. "Well," she went on more briskly, "I've been busy with your colleague, X-117. It's a difficult case. Marriage might help him, though, and I'm sorry the facilities weren't announced earlier. You know, he's too sociable for Level 7, but if he'd been able to marry before the hysterical symptoms appeared, it might have provided a harmless outlet for his sociable impulses. It's not so easy now." Then she glanced up at me and gave what I took to be a winning smile. "Still, don't let's waste our half hour talking about X-117. I've had enough of him recently."

I wanted to hear more about my fellow-officer, but I did not ask her to go on. She had a right to rest, after all. I remained silent, not knowing quite what to say. P-867, however, needs very little co-operation in conversation. She eagerly went on talking.

"You know," she said, "I've had two proposals of marriage through the mediation service. Two shy officers," she giggled, "want to marry me!"

I congratulated her on her success, but this did not seem to satisfy her. "Aren't you jealous?" she asked. "Or are you so sure of your charms that you know I shall refuse my two shy officers? Oh, you naughty X-127!" She gave me an arch look, fluttering her eye-lashes in a coquettish manner.

I failed to see why I was naughty, I was not in the least jealous, and I did not care a damn whom she married, or whether she married at all. But I made some silly remark about how sure I was she would refuse her shy suitors, whoever they were. This seemed to confirm my naughtiness, in her eyes; which meant my interest in her.

Our half hour in the lounge was up at this point, and on parting from P-867 I felt some relief.

I am playing cat and mouse with P-867. She, of course, is the cat.

She wants to marry me. I do not want to marry at all, and if I had felt like marrying at any time I would have chosen N-527. But I have missed my chance there, I admit. Her marriage to E-647 was announced yesterday.

I am trying to escape from P-867 by talking to other people when I visit the lounge—the only alternative is to give up going there, which would be a pity. Yesterday I discovered a quiet girl there, R-747. Eventually, when some children have been born and grown past the kindergarten stage, she will become a teacher—T-747. (The reason TN-237m has already had her title changed is that her job is likely to start in less than a year.) R-747 will instruct children from the age of six or seven onwards. In the meantime, she is preparing instructional material and developing methods of education for use on Level 7. Occasionally, as a reserve officer, she is given odd duties which do not require special training, but she says that the task of preparing for the education of the coming generation is enough by itself to keep her pretty busy.

I said I did not see how this could occupy all her working life for the next six or seven years, so she explained some of the problems to me. "Look," she said, "when you were six years old I expect your grandmother sat you on her knee and told you stories about a good Lord in heaven who rewarded good children, about angels who watched over you when you were asleep, and so on. If you were a naughty boy, then you may have been frightened of going to hell, which was supposed to be a place deep, deep down inside the earth. Now, stories like these——"

Here she was interrupted by P-867, who had been listening to the last part of our conversation. "Stories like those are nonsense anyhow," she objected, "and they interfere with the normal development of the child. I hope you're not going to teach that kind of rubbish to the children down here."

"That's just what I was going to say," replied R-747 quietly. "We can't tell the children that the way to hell is downwards, and to heaven upwards. We'll have to reverse the story: hell will be somewhere up there, and paradise deep inside the earth—deeper than Level 7, even. Or perhaps Level 7 itself will be the new heaven."

P-867 wanted to interrupt again, but I broke in before she did—on purpose, because her constant company was becoming increasingly irksome to me, while the problems raised by R-747 were interesting and provided new food for thought. Addressing R-747, I said: "So what you're trying to do is to create a new mythology, one adapted to fit the facts and supply the needs of Level 7."

P-867 snorted: "But why do we need mythology at all? To hell with all this nonsense!"

"Don't you mean 'to heaven' with it?" I asked; but my little quip reverberated in a sinister way in my mind, so I added crossly: "What do psychologists understand about mythology, anyway?"

This made her angry and she found some excuse to leave us. I cheered up at that, for the creation of myths seemed a fascinating pastime to me, and it was obvious I would not have been able to go on discussing the subject with P-867 around.

Unfortunately our time in the lounge was up a minute later, so I had to break off my talk with R-747.

APRIL 25

I was indeed lucky yesterday. A few minutes after finishing that entry in my diary I walked around to the lounge and had R-747 all to myself for the whole half hour. P-867 did not put in an appearance, so we were able to carry on our discussion of mythology quite undisturbed.

Today it was not so good. P-867 reappeared and tried to keep me at her side by giving me a detailed progress report on X-117, who seems to be getting better. But as we were leaving the lounge R-747 was able to hand me a sheet of paper, asking me to let her have it back the next time we met.

I have just finished reading what is written on it: a story for the children of the future generations. I find it a very interesting story, and here it is, copied word for word:

Gamma, Alpha and Little Ch-777

Once upon a time, many years ago, there lived on Level 7 a little boy called Ch-777 (Ch for Child). He was a nice little boy and a good pupil, but he had one strange weakness: he was curious to know what went on above him, above our good Level 7.

"Tell me," he used to say, "please tell me what goes on up there." And when his parents heard him ask that they were frightened, for they did not want even to speak of the hell up there. But the little boy kept on asking: "Tell me, please tell me what goes on up there." So one day they told him.

The higher you went up from Level 7, they said, the closer you came to Him whose name must not be mentioned. He could not be seen, and He could not be heard, and He could not be touched, and He could not be smelled, but up there His power was infinite. If anybody went near His kingdom, said the parents, he would be killed at once by His invisible servants.

At this Ch-777 became very frightened, and many days went by without his asking a single silly question. But after a while his curiosity got the better of him again, and this time he asked his teacher: "Tell me what goes on up there."

The teacher, who knew more about the world outside Level 7 than little Ch-777's parents did, told him that He who ruled up there was called—and even she was afraid to pronounce His name aloud—St 90. She called Him 'Saint 90', for she did not want to say His real name, which was (she said in a whisper) Strontium 90.

Saint 90 was the omnipotent master of death and destruction. He was the supreme ruler of the upper world, and to carry out His evil designs He had servants who obeyed His every command—wicked little devils whose touch was deadly too.

Such were the two small devils called Alpha and Gamma. Their job was to wander around in the upper world, trying to find somebody to kill. They got very bored doing this, because the upper world had long before been conquered by St 90 and His servants, and now there was no living creature left to kill.

"Would they kill me too," asked Ch-777, "if I went to the upper world?"

"Of course they would, you silly boy," the teacher said. "And probably they would catch you before you even got there."

After this Ch-777 did not ask anyone any more questions. But he could not forget the story about the upper world. Every night he dreamt about little Alpha and little Gamma, who appeared as two lovely sisters of his own age who wanted him to play with them. Before long he really believed that these two devils were just two friendly little girls.

Now he stopped paying attention to what was going on around him on good Level 7. He became bored with all the interesting things that were happening, he became a bad pupil, and one day . . . he disappeared.

How he managed to get out, nobody knew. But he left a letter saying that he was going up to join the little girls Alpha and Gamma.

Nobody ever saw him again. No doubt he was killed by Alpha or Gamma, or by some other devil, on his way up.

And this, children, is the moral of the story: Do not think of the world above you. Be happy here. If you are curious to know what happens above Level 7, think of poor Ch-777 who paid for his curiosity with his life.

I think this story is quite good in its way, though it has room for improvement. For instance, why blame Ch-777's sense of curiosity for his tragic end? It could be suggested that the devils Alpha and Gamma, on the orders of St 90, entered his head and made him mad enough to want to go up where their master would be able to devour him.

I think this version is more frightening. I shall suggest it to R-747. It could be used to make children obey adults' commands: if they don't, they can be warned, Alpha and Gamma will enter their heads and make them go up to be killed by St 90.

APRIL 26

I gave R-747 her story back today and suggested my alternative version. She agreed that mine probably was more frightening and better as a mythological story, but still preferred her original because it kept closer to the facts and so was of greater educational value. P-867, who was listening (rather quietly, for a change), remarked maliciously: "I think Alpha and Gamma have entered your heads already! The whole idea's insane."

I could not deny that her remark was sharp, but I did not let her see that I had enjoyed it.

An atomic energy officer, AE-327, had been listening to our conversation too. He asked to see R-747's manuscript, and after glancing through it made a few technical comments. First, he said, she was wrong about the chemical symbol of Strontium, which was Sr and not St. "So there's nothing saintly about Strontium," he said. Then he added that, unfortunately for the nice story, Strontium 90's half-life (the time which elapsed before its radioactivity fell to half its original value) was only twenty-five years. "So your saint would be a very short-lived one," he said with a laugh. "Why not take Plutonium 239, an isotope with a half-life of 24,100 years? Better still, choose Thorium 232: that has a half-life of 13,900 million years!"

"That would be splendid," remarked P-867 mischievously. "With the symbol 'Th' it's really theological."

AE-327 smiled and went on to object to R-747's devils too. "Gamma rays and alpha particles aren't really as alike as the sisters of the story," he said. "What's more, Strontium 90 emits *beta* particles, not alpha. If you've got to have alpha particles, you'll have to make Plutonium 239 or Thorium 232 the villain of the piece. As for gamma rays——"

Here I, rather impolitely, interrupted my learned colleague. I could not stand his pedantic objections, which seemed to pour even colder water on the idea of a new mythology than P-867's cynical remarks. I said that stories for children need not be scientifically accurate. If they were, they would not be stories!

It was time for us to leave the lounge, but before we parted I promised to give R-747 a story of my own next time we met.

I have now written and revised my story. Here it is.

The Story of the Mushroom

Here is a story from the Sacred Tape which can be heard by any child who pushes the ST button.

Once upon a time, many years ago, people did not live on Level 7, but far above, on the crust of the earth. They had no natural roof over their heads, and they used to be made wet by water falling on them, or burned by a huge fiery ball which was suspended over them for about twelve hours each day. This made their life very hard.

For a long time the people were very miserable because of the falling water and the fiery ball, not to mention the violent air currents which blew with the strength of a million electric

74

fans. Little by little, however, they learned to erect roofs over their heads, and even to build small boxes to live in.

They taught these skills to their children, and the children taught them to *their* children, and so on for many generations. And as time went by the people grew better and better at making their boxes. Before long the little boxes gave place to huge, high ones—some as high as our dining-room is long, and some even higher than that.

But this did not satisfy them. They no longer wanted just to be protected from the wet and the burning ball and the air currents: they wanted to go higher and higher. So they invented gadgets which made them able to walk around in the air, and they thought that the higher they went the better they were. After some time they had gadgets which went up so high in the air that people standing on the earth could no longer see them.

But even this was not enough for them. They had shown that they could build big things and could go high in the air. Now they wanted to take a very *small* thing and make it change itself into a giant, so that it would grow high into the air all by itself.

So they found a small and fragile thing that grew out of the earth, something called a mushroom. It was so small and weak that a child's foot was enough to crush it to pieces. But unless they could transform this tiny mushroom into the biggest and strongest thing on earth, the people would not consider themselves happy.

So the most learned ones put their heads together, and thought and worked, and worked and thought, until one day they succeeded. The mushroom began to grow!

There was a big celebration, and the people who had discovered how to make the mushroom grow became very important.

And the mushroom grew and grew and grew. Before long it was higher than the highest boxes. And still it went on growing. Now it reached the flying gadgets. And still it grew.

But something was happening which the people had not intended: as the mushroom grew it emitted a strong smell. Few people noticed it to start with, but as the mushroom got bigger the odour became stronger, and more and more people began to smell it. Some could not endure it and became ill and died. In spite of that the others put up with the bad smell, happy that their mushroom was growing so large.

As time went by, the mushroom grew so big, and its smell grew so strong, that some people began to be afraid of it. So they looked for a place to hide. There was no place they could find on earth where they could not smell the mushroom, so they started to dig down.

Down they dug, down, down, down . . . until they arrived at Level 7. And when they got to Level 7 they could not smell the mushroom any more.

But the thing they had escaped from was still growing and growing, swelling and covering the whole earth with shadow and stink, until one day—it burst!

In a split second the mushroom exploded into millions of little pieces, and the air carried the particles into the people's boxes, into their flying gadgets, everywhere. And everyone who was touched by a particle, or who smelled the bad odour, died. And it was not long before there was not a single person left alive on the surface of the earth. Only the few who had dug into the earth survived. And you, children, are their offspring.

And this is the moral . . .

No, I do not feel like adding a moral. I wonder what R-747 will think of my story.

APRIL 28

I spent much of yesterday writing an introduction to my diary. Why did the idea of writing it occur to me yesterday?

I think my mythological 'Story of the Mushroom' must have stirred me to think again about the significance of my situation.

The little story seems to justify the descent all right, but the introduction speaks of 'dungeons' in a way far from favourable to Level 7.

How do I really feel about it? Am I adjusted to Level 7, or do I still feel imprisoned? Do I *know* how I feel? *Can* a man know how he feels?

My feelings do not seem at all clear: one day I make up a story suggesting that those who descend into the earth are the *luck*y few, and the next day this story makes me reflect on the shattering experience of being locked in the dungeons of Level 7. I wonder what comes next!

No, it seems that feeling and knowing are two different things, and that one cannot know how, or even what, one feels.

R-747 liked my story. She thinks she will be able to use it when the children who will be born get old enough.

The Sacred Tape, ST, seems to her an excellent idea. She thinks it will be a useful means of education: "We can't use books to teach people on Level 7," she said. "They would take up so much space, and anyway they're an outdated method of imparting information: only one person can read a book at a time, whereas there's no limit to the number of people who can listen to a loudspeaker. It'll be most convenient to have a Sacred Tape instead of a Sacred Book—especially since the stories in the conventional sacred books don't fit the conditions of Level 7."

P-867, set on finding snags in anything R-747 and I are mutually concerned with, remarked that there was a danger of confusion in the similarity of 'ST' for Sacred Tape and 'St' for Saint, alias (and she dropped her voice to a whisper, glancing round her in mock apprehension) Strontium.

We had to admit her point, but I minimised it by pointing

77

out that although the children might hear references to 'ST' they would not hear people talking about 'St'—it would be pronounced 'Saint' or 'Strontium' as the case might be. And if most teaching was to be done by loudspeaker they would get the spoken words clear in their heads before meeting them in their abbreviated, and possibly confusing, written form.

People are getting married down here at an increasingly fast rate. The marriages are always announced on the loud-speaker, but I have stopped counting them. They go on taking place, that's all I know.

P-867 comes out most days with some new story about proposals made to her, either directly or through the mediation service. This does not interest me and I no longer go through the motions of asking her who her suitors are or whether she will say yes to one of them. I know it is myself she has designs on.

MAY 1

Last night I had a horrible dream. And it was so vivid, I can remember its details just as if it were a real experience.

I dreamed that I was walking along a street in a city—a large place of several million inhabitants. Suddenly the sky began to darken and I had that sensation, which one often gets in dreams, that something terrible was going to happen. People were running past me, pointing up at the sky and dodging into doorways for shelter. I took cover in a big, solid-looking building, and found myself in a large hall with tall windows—some sort of place for public assemblies—together with many other people. Just as I entered the hall there was a dazzling, sustained glare of light from outside, and I had several drawn-out seconds to see the frightened faces of the

78

people round me before the sound of the explosion came and darkness closed in on us again.

Now it was lighter. I was standing at one of the windows, looking out towards the centre of the city. To my horror, where I expected to see a mass of huge buildings there was nothing: what had been there was erased from the surface of the earth. I remember wondering how all that concrete, steel and glass could possibly have disappeared. The buildings in the centre of the city had been considerably taller than those farther out and had dominated the skyline. But now I was shocked to find that I could see right across the city to smaller buildings which should have been hidden from view. Between me and them lay two or three square miles of flat, dead ground.

Everybody in the room seemed as horrified as myself. Nobody said anything. We just stood there looking at each other and occasionally turning to stare out of the windows.

Then, without any visible transition (as frequently happens in dreams), a change came over the people. I suddenly noticed that their faces and hands were a yellowish colour. The yellow turned to brown, and now they were sinking down on the floor, their flesh changing into lifeless rubber. They lay all around me, still moving their limbs; but gradually their movements became slower and slower . . . were hardly perceptible . . . looked like the last movements of crushed worms. Then they stopped! Now I was surrounded by grotesque brown rubber dummies.

I raised my hands to cover my eyes, and my heart stood still as I saw that they were yellow. Slowly their colour darkened to brown. . . .

I woke up at this point and was spared the rest.

Or was I? Was this nightmare just a dream? Had it not an element of real premonition in it? Was it not a prophecy?

I know it is absurd to explain dreams in such a way. But

79

this one seems so closely connected with our times and situation that it weighs heavily on my mind.

That empty hole where the huge buildings used to be, those bodies that looked like rubber, their last worm-like movements, my hands turning brown. . . .

If only I had a God to cry to!

The dream has had a bad effect on me. I am upset again and my spirits are as low as ever. I told P-867 so today and described the dream to her. She is a psychologist, after all.

She said I was showing quasi-hysterical symptoms. She thought that those mythological stories of R-747's and mine were upsetting my emotional stability. There was a connection, she suggested, between the mushroom in my story and my nightmare. I had to admit she might be right. "But the roots lie deeper," she added. "There's some more fundamental anxiety in you somewhere. It may be due, partly at least, to the fact that you don't lead a normal life for a healthy man of your age."

Does she want to scare me into marriage? If I could be sure that marriage would help me over my ups and downs, or rather my downs and downs, I would marry right away. I would even marry P-867, if a psychologist mate is the best sort to have.

I wish somebody could advise me about that. P-867 could, if she were not personally involved.

I really do not know what to do, but I am sure I cannot take many more downs. There must be a limit to mental suffering, just as there is a limit to the distance humans can dig into the earth. Seven levels down is the physical limit. How many can the spirit endure?

X-117 came back today. He looks emaciated and pale, but behaves quite normally. He is rather silent. Nobody asks him about the treatment.

I asked P-867 about it. She told me it was psychoanalysis, combined with some drugs which speed up the therapy a lot. She said X-117 is perfectly all right now and can fulfil his duties.

But I am sure there *is* something different about him. I mean that besides losing a bit of weight and colour he has changed in some way. I told P-867 I thought so, but she laughed at the idea and said it was just a layman's imagination. She added, wistfully: "You haven't been looking so well yourself lately."

She is probably right. I wonder if I shall be the next patient of P-867 and her colleagues. I would prefer to be her husband, if that would spare me being her patient.

There will be no need to be either if only I can get rid of the gloomy thoughts which creep into my mind all the time.

Today I tried to lose myself again in the mental game of inventing new myths for the coming generation on Level 7. I thought about it a good deal and then discussed it with R-747 in the lounge.

While I am busy speculating and talking about such things I forget my own predicament. Maybe it is dangerous to escape from reality in this way—P-867 would certainly say it is —but the practice helps me, at least while I am indulging in it.

I suggested to R-747 a few general principles which she

might keep in mind when she is creating new myths and stories. Here are some of them.

High is bad, low is good. Open space is harmful; enclosed space is beneficial. Vast distances are the product of a sick or perverse imagination; being content with the physical limits of one's level is normal and admirable. The quest for variety in life is wicked; sticking to one's job and being satisfied with little entertainment is good citizenship.

R-747 thought these principles would be quite helpful and said she would use them when she wrote some more stories.

P-867 interrupted us as usual. I cannot get rid of her during my discussions with R-747.

MAY 5

Last night I had another 'atomic' dream.

I was standing with my parents on the corner of two streets in my home town. The sky above us was full of strange flying objects which, though they did not look like conventional aircraft or missiles, had obviously something to do with atomic warfare. I was watching with particular interest some big spherical objects which floated slowly through the air, surrounded by smaller, swift-moving machines with wings. I was not at all sure what these glittering little machines were doing. I had the vague impression that their swift flight around the big balls was for the purpose of protecting us from them, but my mind was more taken up with the spectacle which these various objects presented—they resembled a cluster of planets floating through space, each one with its satellite moons. But it was clear that this strange universe was man-made; it was too near the earth to be anything else. The big, apparently clumsy spheres—or were they just balloons?— moved slowly over our heads with the little winged objects circling them incessantly. Now they made me think of huge,

82

ponderous bears surrounded by packs of small but alert wolves.

The sky was brightly lit—it was not clear what time of day it was—and as my gaze wandered farther out into space I noticed for the first time some white tracks in the blue, the sort made by jets at high altitudes. It was as if, while I looked, new forms of life were springing into existence above me. Perhaps 'life' is not quite the word, for I knew that the things I was watching were inanimate; but their movements made me think of them as living things. I was standing there staring at them, so fascinated that I had forgotten all about my parents and where we were supposed to be going, when all at once, with a suddenness which I recall with horrid vividness but can find no words to express, the whole scene was blotted out in a blinding flash of light.

I knew at once that an atomic explosion had taken place over our heads. The corner on which we were standing was rather exposed, and the nearest building big enough to offer any protection was a good fifty yards off. I dashed away towards it, shouting to my parents to follow, even though I knew it was no use. We might have done better to throw ourselves flat on the ground where we stood.

Next moment I was lying on the ground. I thought: 'Now I am being killed.' I knew it as a crystal-clear fact: my death was inevitable and occurring at that very moment. Yet my consciousness was still clear, and I summoned every mental resource in my effort to keep it so. It was purely mental effort, for I was aware of no physical sensations at all. The body seemed to have stopped feeling. But the mental effort was enormous—to be, to be!

Within that single moment of strain the problem of the immortality of my soul was folded. I was aware of it in my dream very clearly. But I also knew that the outcome of my fight would solve the universal problem of the immortality of the human soul. In fighting my own fight for survival, I fought for the whole of humanity as well.

I was still fighting when I came out of the dream. And I lay half-awake for some time, trying to decide what the struggle had meant. Had I retained my hold on consciousness after my body had been disintegrated, or had I woken before my physical destruction was complete? I could not decide.

After a while I woke up completely and gave up my philosophical meditations. It was time to attend to the more practical matters of today. But all day the memory of the dream has kept slipping into my thoughts.

Am I going to have any more 'atomic' dreams, I wonder? Can't I look forward to peace of mind even when I am asleep?

MAY 6

I am trying to decide on the best cure for my low spirits. Possibly it will have to be a compromise.

For one thing, I want to carry on my talks with R-747. They may be harmful, but they act as a sort of drug that gives me relief while I am actually taking it. At present the relief does not last long enough, but the process of taking the talk-drug can be stretched. Like chewing-gum.

On the other hand, marriage might counteract my dreams. If I could stop having 'atomic' nightmares without having to give up thinking about myths and things, that would be splendid.

I think I should take P-867 as my mate. I do not care for her much, admittedly, but perhaps this is an advantage. To like anybody a lot on Level 7 would only lead to trouble. Down here we do not have the facilities for close contact between married couples which people enjoy up on the surface. To be really in love down here would mean daily torments of separation. Up there one hour's privacy a day for a newly-wed couple would be considered cruelty. On Level 7 restricted privacy is a necessity, so the less a person cares for his mate the better.

That suggests another principle for R-747 to use in her stories: Do not care for other people too much, especially if they belong to your own family. I must tell her that one.

If I offer to marry P-867 I think she may put less obstacles in the way of my talks with R-747, which is another point in favour of the idea. To make sure, I think I should stipulate it as a condition of the marriage. P-867 is sensible enough to realise that I only talk with R-747 for the sake of the mental pleasure it gives me.

As my mate, P-867 may be able to help me psychologically without treating me as a patient. I need her professional skill unprofessionally exercised.

Looking at it all round, I am forced to conclude that P-867 is the best possible match for me in the present circumstances —the circumstances of Level 7, which is the best of all possible worlds.

Well, perhaps it isn't—the world, I mean—but the marriage seems all right.

The very idea of the bargain makes me feel better already.

MAY 7

Today I suggested to P-867 that we should get married, but I stressed at the same time that I wanted to be free to talk to R-747 during my half hours in the lounge.

P-867 promptly accepted both my proposal and the reservation. She seemed happy and wanted us to press the red button together and announce our decision at once. This was all right with me. Now I am waiting for the private loudspeaker to say when the ceremony will take place, and I will finish writing this entry when the message has come through.

I have received the message: "Marriage Service calling X-127. Your marriage with P-867 has been approved. The ceremony will take place today in the Marriage Room at 7 p.m. sharp. Kindly press the red button and confirm that you have received and understood this message."

I was just doing so when X-107 walked into the room. He must have guessed from the expression on my face that the message I was acknowledging was no ordinary one, for he smiled and raised a questioning eyebrow. When I told him I was marrying P-867 this very evening, he congratulated me warmly and said he thought I had made a very wise decision.

I am glad he approves, because of course we shall remain room-mates and I shall still spend many more hours with him than with my future wife—a consoling thought, somehow.

MAY 8

Yesterday evening I met P-867 at the appointed time and place, and a couple of minutes later we were out, duly married and with the letters 'm' fixed to our identity badges.

We smiled when we saw how our names had grown, and decided on the spot that between ourselves we would forget the ponderous P-867m and X-127m and call each other P and X for short.

Then P suggested that we should follow up the official ceremony with an unofficial celebration. We were right in the dining-room, where the second shift was in the middle of its meal and I could not think what P had in mind. She drew me mysteriously into a corner where we would not disturb the diners, fished in her pocket, said: "Here's how we'll celebrate," and produced—a small bar of chocolate.

It seems that she happened to have this chocolate on her when she was ordered down to Level 7. She had kept it all this time for some special occasion, and now the occasion had arrived. She broke the bar in two and gave me the bigger piece.

I raised it as if it were a glass and proposed the toast: "To you and me!"

86

"To X and P!" she rhymed. Then we ate the chocolate, nibbling bits off and chewing them slowly as if we were sipping at a wine of old and rare vintage.

This is rather what the experience was like, in fact. We had been down here long enough to forget completely what ordinary food tasted like. The stuff we had grown used to had hardly any flavour, and we ate it automatically and without interest—feeding had become a sort of reflex action at certain hours of the day.

As a result, the chocolate P produced was like some rich, exotic delicacy to our bored palates, and we both prolonged the eating as long as we could. The chocolate lasted ten minutes; and then we had to part, as the second shift had finished at the table and we were getting in people's way.

We do not know our hours of privacy yet, but the loudspeaker will tell us in due course, so there is no need to worry about making dates. The Marriage Service will work out the best time, taking into account our working hours and the requirements of the other married couples.

I am sure our next meeting will be planned in the best possible way.

MAY 10

My honeymoon has had to be postponed. Instead of meeting P, I have just spent forty-eight hours in hospital. It really is funny. I think it is the first amusing thing that has happened since I came down to Level 7.

My case history is quite simple. After writing that last entry in my diary I went on duty in the Operations Room. I had not been there long before my stomach started to feel bad. Soon the unpleasant sensations became quite a fierce pain, and I decided I should have to do something about it. Such a thing had never happened to me before.

I pushed the red button and asked for help and instructions. They worked fast. Five minutes later X-117 came in to take my place and the loudspeaker told me to go to my room until they came to escort me to the hospital. I hardly had time to stretch out on my bed before two nurses arrived (despite my pains I noticed that one of them wore an 'm' and the other did not) and helped me across to the ward. Within a quarter of an hour of having sent my S.O.S., I was tucked up in a hospital bed.

There was nothing unusual about the ward. It was small, of course, like most of the rooms here, with only five beds beside mine, all of them empty. So I had the lady doctor, M-227m, all to myself. She took my temperature, looked at my tongue, poked me, asked me a couple of questions, and finally told me I had upset my stomach by eating something unsuitable.

I might have guessed: the chocolate. When I told her I had eaten some she laughed and said: "That's it. I'm glad there's nothing wrong with the food you *ought* to have been eating." It was not that the chocolate was bad, she explained; but my stomach had grown unused to tackling that sort of food. "You're already a Level 7 man," she said. "You can't digest that kind of thing any more." Then she added: "By the way, where did you get your chocolate? I wouldn't mind a piece myself—a very small piece, of course."

When I told her that it had been my wedding feast and that it was all gone, she had a good laugh and said: "So you're suffering from marriage pains! Serves you right! I suppose your bride will be arriving any moment now—she ate some too, didn't she?"

But P did not appear. Her digestion must be better than mine. What's more, she gave me the bigger piece of chocolate.

The doctor found me some pills which purged my stomach and after that the pains soon wore off. I felt a bit weak and dizzy, though, and still do.

I was quite sorry to leave the ward this afternoon. It may

sound odd, but I really enjoyed being there. The whole business was so comical: a stomach upset by a chocolate toast after a wedding ceremony, and then a 'honeymoon' spent in a hospital bed.

I enjoyed the pain too. This may sound downright perverse, but it is true. I enjoyed it because it broke the deadening routine. It made me feel that I was still alive, alive to sensations which were felt by people up there on the surface.

More than that, the pain proved my identity to me in a way that my symbol, X-127m, cannot do. Somebody once said: "I think, therefore I am." But it seems to me that thinking makes you forget your own personality, it dissolves your individuality in the impersonal universe of spirit. But feeling, feeling an acute pain, tells you that *you* are. It makes you aware of yourself as nothing else does. There is nothing universal about the feeling of pain; it is the most private of experiences.

Though I am still weak, my state of physical emptiness is a good one and conducive to meditation. Those pills seem to have purged my mind as well as my body. My depression has gone, I feel much more cheerful. I don't even want to discuss myths with R-747. For the time being, my addiction to that spiritual drug is cured.

This is the first occasion on which I have felt really grateful to P. But for her persistent efforts to get me to marry her, and but for her piece of chocolate, I should still be going round in my black mood.

The pangs of marriage certainly did me good. I only hope it will not be undone by marriage's other aspects.

MAY 12

I am quite well now. And a proper married man too.

P seemed quite worried about my stomach trouble when we met again yesterday. This was perfectly natural in a

89

newly-wedded woman, and it prompted me to ask her why she had not visited me in the hospital. She said she had been told no visitors were allowed. Apparently the rule is quite inflexible.

I wonder why this should be. I suppose it is considered better to hide sick people away, not only for reasons of hygiene, but to preserve the morale of their healthy friends. It is always depressing to visit a person in the hospital, and if you do not see for yourself how ill a patient is you are more likely to assume that no news (or the vague information which doctors begrudgingly allow you) is good news.

Incidentally, P had a touch of indigestion herself, as might have been expected, but it was not enough to stop her working.

I find her more pleasant now. In conversation her tongue is not so sharp. Indeed she talks less altogether.

Our time of privacy is 16.15 to 17.00 hours each day—4.15 to 5.00 in the afternoon. We are lucky in this respect: some people get it at 4.15 a.m. On second thoughts, I suppose it would not make much difference. The working hours of many of the crew—myself included—are scheduled on a 24-hour basis, and down here 'day' and 'night' mean very little. Regular private meetings with P will enliven my daily routine, which is all to the good, not to mention the other benefits which marriage should bring with it—even on Level 7.

The desire to discuss mythologies with R-747 has not returned. As a matter of fact, I have hardly spoken to her since I came out of hospital. Yesterday and today I spent my time in the lounge chatting with P. And P actually tried to draw R-747 into the conversation. A strange metamorphosis in our relationship.

Today I have had an interesting talk with X-107 about marriage on Level 7.

I was humming a tune, I think, and my obvious good spirits must have started a train of thought in my room-mate's head. "It seems to work all right even on Level 7," he remarked.

This rather cryptic statement got no reply and clearly needed elucidation. "The institution of marriage, I mean," he went on. "You know, I had the gravest misgivings about it. It seemed to me that it should have been abolished altogether."

"Why so?" I asked. "What about the future of the human race? You wouldn't like to see Level 7 die out in a generation, would you?"

"Of course not," X-107 said. "But monogamous marriage isn't the only way of preserving the species. Free love would have done it just as well. What's more, it would have been more convenient: there wouldn't have been the problem of scheduling hours of privacy to fit in with working hours. Nobody pretends that marriage down here is anything more than a means of providing a future generation—there are no private households, no family life—so why preserve the old formalities?"

I agreed that the arrangement was very conservative, but pointed out (as X-107 always used to do) that there must be a good reason for it. Perhaps it was to prevent jealousy, I suggested. That was a sentiment which could be terribly disruptive in the rather claustrophobic atmosphere of Level 7.

X-107 thought about that for a moment or two, and then asked me whether I would feel jealous about my mate. I said no, I would not; but other people might. X-107 said he thought most other people on Level 7 would not either. "You're probably quite the opposite of an exception," he said.

"I'd be surprised if an absence of jealous tendencies wasn't one of the main things they looked for in the people they selected for this place.

"Still," he went on, "monogamous marriage seems to work all right down here, and so far they've had no difficulty in finding times when couples can be together in private, so I suppose things are best as they are. If free enterprise were the rule, there might be too much competition in the field; people would spend too much time thinking about it, and their work would suffer."

"Besides," I added, "free enterprise and equality aren't often found together. And equality is the basis of democracy, and democracy's finest flower is Level 7."

I did not mean that very seriously, but X-107 nodded his head in solemn agreement. Level 7 retained its position as the best of all possible levels.

MAY 14

P seems to be almost in love with me. I wonder if she would feel jealous about me. I told her about my discussion with X-107 and she said she had credited him with more sense. I tried to defend him, and in the end she agreed to give him the benefit of the doubt. She ended by saying that he himself should get married. Then he would talk less nonsense.

Marriages go on taking place at a steady rate. One sees more and more people at meal-times with the 'm' attached to their badges, and every day there are fresh announcements over the loudspeaker: engineers, doctors, nurses, food-supply officers, wastage officers, air-supply men, atomic energy officers, loudspeaker officers, psychologists, quite a number of reserve officers and many others have paired up. X-117's room-mate, X-137, has married too. That leaves only two bachelors out of the four of us.

The 'Know Thy Level' talks finished today. In the sum-

92

ming up of the series great stress was laid on the significance of our position on Level 7, the deepest and safest place of all.

The reason for that privileged position is the function of Level 7. At the centre of everything is PBX Command, which is the offensive branch of our military power. "Attack," the speaker explained, "is the best form of defence." That is the reason why Level 7 is so deep in the earth: it can hit the enemy and devastate his country while all the time remaining out of his reach.

What he said made me think afresh about my personal position on Level 7. It really is a pretty significant one. *I* push the buttons, and most of the others are down here to supply the necessities of life for *me:* to provide me with air, food, energy and so on, and to look after my physical and mental health.

Of course, everybody down here is necessary. Without their services we push-button officers could not do a thing. And X-117's illness has proved the importance of people like P, who provide nothing in the material sense but stand by in case anything goes wrong with our minds. Still, the knowledge that Level 7 centres round the push-button function, that it houses the Push-Button X Command, in fact, gives me a feeling of importance.

There must still be the Command itself, naturally, whatever it may be. I have never noticed anybody wearing a badge with 'C' on it, nor have any 'C' marriages been announced. I wonder who and how many the commanders are.

At the end of today's talk the speaker announced a new series which is to start tomorrow: 'Know Other Levels'. This may prove more interesting, for the 'Know Thy Level' series mostly confirmed and explained things we knew about already from daily experience, while the new talks may introduce us to worlds unknown.

The 'Know Other Levels' series has begun with the next level up and will work towards the surface. Today we were told about Level 6.

Level 6 is for the Push-Button Y Command. Our PBX buttons are for attack. The PBY buttons control the defensive branch of the country's military power. Although PBY Command is in a sense less significant than ours—its actions cannot be so decisive—it requires a larger personnel and far more complicated machinery.

The task of PBY Command is to intercept enemy rockets and destroy them before they reach their destinations. And since an attack may come as a surprise, it has to be on the watch all the time. So it collects, classifies and remembers innumerable details of aerial activity. There are huge electronic computers whose task it is to collate two kinds of information: flight schedules, which are sent to Level 6 from aircraft and rocket bases up and down the country; and details of actual flights obtained from radar reports. If all is as it should be, there are no actual flights which cannot be collated with the schedules already received. But if radar reports a flight which has *not* been scheduled, a computer singles it out at once as suspect. It feeds the necessary information into a second computer, which takes over the tracking of the unscheduled flying object and, on the basis of further radar data, accurately calculates its speed, altitude and direction of flight.

If and when—and this need take no more than a few minutes—the suspect object is identified as an enemy missile, PBY Command takes its first positive action. One of our opposite numbers pushes the button which commands the area over which the enemy object is flying, and so releases ground-to-air interceptors. (There is no double control or additional supervision up there.) The interceptors, which are fitted with small atomic warheads, are radio-controlled by the tracking computer. The button-pusher only indicates the area of action, he does not aim the interceptors. But he can see whether they are successful, because he has a viewing screen, rather like ours, which shows him what is happening.

I find all this very interesting, because it is so much more complicated than the workings of PBX Command. Our intercontinental rockets are all aimed in advance at their immobile strategic targets. All we have to do is press the buttons which send them on their predetermined way. But PBY Command first has to keep an eye on the countless flights which are going on all over the country, and then, when it has singled out a flight that should *not* be going on, must aim at a small, very rapidly moving target.

Of course, it is the computers and other machines which do most of the work, but this does not mean that the staff of Level 6 can be as small as ours. There is so much more machinery to be looked after that they need a personnel of 2,000—four times the number on Level 7. And in spite of this, the speaker said today, many of the auxiliary services are worse manned than down here, and the crew do not enjoy quite the same degree of comfort, though their level is intended to be as self-sufficient as ours. The fact that Level 6 is only 3,000 feet underground, too, is because of the physical difficulty of constructing a deeper level big enough to house everything.

I do not know whether it was to make us feel privileged and contented, or what, but the speaker kept saying, both by implication and by direct assertion, that Level 7 was more important than Level 6 as well as more comfortable. We were told—and I see no reason to doubt it—that the country relied far more on PBX Command, its offensive arm, than on the defensive PBY Command. This is because it is very doubtful whether the defence system could work quickly enough to deal with inter-continental missiles approaching us at the speed of thousands of miles an hour. Added to this, we do not

95

know what gadgets the enemy's missiles may be fitted with —to deflect or destroy any interceptors which manage to come near them. "Our own offensive missiles are equipped with devices against enemy interceptors," we were told.

The chances that we shall be able to destroy the majority of the attacking missiles outside our territory are very small. But even if we are incredibly lucky, and only ten per cent of the enemy rockets reach our country, we shall still be badly devastated. And even if many rockets out of this ten per cent do not hit their predetermined targets, the radioactive fallout (for the atomic bombs will explode even if intercepted) may make the country uninhabitable for some time.

For how long? I wondered. The loudspeaker did not say.

MAY 16

The talk about Level 6 and the PBY Command has aroused a lot of interest on our own level.

People's feelings seem to be ambivalent. On the one hand, we feel superior. Firstly, because we are inferior—deeper in the earth. Secondly, because our country relies mainly on the offensive branch. Thirdly, because we are a smaller group.

On the other hand, though, we have to admit that the operations on Level 6 are more intricate and require greater skill. The PBY officers probably have higher technical qualifications, and in that sense they must be superior. So argues X-107, and he is probably right.

We also feel both a liking and an enmity for Level 6. They are a branch of the military forces, entrusted, like ourselves, with the country's safety—so we feel friendly towards them. But they are also a *different* branch of those forces—so there is a feeling of competition.

Of course, all these feelings are really just speculations as to possible feelings. Actual feelings are rather difficult to have when one knows so little about their object. For the crew of

Level 6 are 1,400 feet above our heads, and there is no communication between us.

Or is there none? It seems to me there must be. If the enemy attacked, it would be PBY Command which would know about it first. They must have some way of telling us.

This is an exciting idea: contact with outside. Or rather, with a more outside inside. But there is no point in guessing about that kind of thing when you have no information to go on. Perhaps today's talk will say something about it.

The talk was about Level 6 again, but communications were not mentioned. What we did learn was that they are not yet kept below ground all the time. They spend a fortnight down, and then they are replaced and spend a fortnight at a camp near the entrance to the underground before coming down again.

This means that there must be at least 4,000 men and women trained for PBY Command, because there have to be as many people spending their two weeks above as there are manning the level.

But it also means that the people on Level 6 can see daylight and. . . .

No, better not think about that. Anyway, the system has its snags. As X-107 pointed out to me, when war starts the people on Level 6 at that moment will stay there, and the other 2,000 will have to find refuge on a higher, less secure level, or even stay on the surface.

The thought of that should make us feel superior again, I suppose, though the idea of spending two weeks down and two weeks up is most attractive. As far as I could gather from the talk, the Level 6 crew live more or less as surface creatures who come down at regular intervals to work as one might go off on a business trip. It has not been necessary for their social life below ground—marriage, for instance—to be organised as ours is, though presumably that will come if and when Level 6 is sealed off.

97

X-107 has suggested that the life of the Level 6 crew is arranged in this way not simply for convenience: according to him, the half-up, half-down life is as necessary to them as it is out of the question for us. "We're the most important military branch because our action is offensive," he said, "and offensive action isn't directly concerned with what's going on in *our* country, so it isn't necessary for us to keep in touch with the surface. More than that, contact of any kind with the world up there might upset us in our work by making us sentimental about the crust of the earth, which it may be our duty to lay waste. PBY Command, on the other hand, has the task of protecting the surface from attack, and the more the crew of Level 6 can see of the earth, the keener they'll be to do their job well. Also there's not so much point in sealing them off for security, because—as the talk said—it's doubtful whether their operations will be very effective anyhow."

This argument seemed sound enough to me. There really are considerable differences between the two commands, even though the talks have tried to stress the links between Level 6 and ourselves. Today the speaker emphasised the fact that Levels 6 and 7 are the military nerve-centres of our country, and that all the other levels are for civilians only. In the functional sense, broadly speaking, we are one unit.

This is the reason why the two levels were organised along such similar lines, we were told. And though Level 6 is 1,400 feet nearer the surface—for purely technical reasons—it is in the same area. In fact, it is directly above our heads, which makes us close together in the physical sense. (I think there *must* be some very close communication between the two levels. Otherwise why locate them in the same area?) Moreover, there is only *one* Level 6, as there is one Level 7. Other levels, the speaker told us, do not have this characteristic: they are dispersed in several units, the number of which varies from level to level in a way which will be explained to us in a later talk.

This sounds interesting. I look forward to hearing what happens on the other five levels.

P does not understand why I am so interested in the 'Know Other Levels' talks. She seems to find them rather boring. I get the impression that even psychology has lost some of its fascination for her. Her main interest now is myself—as her husband.

Perhaps I should not be surprised at this—it is the way women often behave. They can concentrate all their life around the life of somebody else, around one special person. As long as P has me, or thinks she has me, she does not mind anything else, is not interested in other levels, feels quite happy on Level 7.

I wonder how she would react if the loudspeaker suddenly announced that we were all to go back up to the surface. Would it make a great difference to her?

If P's interest in psychological problems has waned, mine has grown. Maybe her influence has brought this about: perhaps she has transferred her professional interests to me and so somehow got them out of her own system. It may well be so, for we are together a great deal. Not only does she never miss—or allow me to miss—the daily meetings which we, as a married couple, are entitled to; but she also monopolises all my time in the lounge (not that I particularly want to talk to R-747 these days) and often finds ways of seeing me on other occasions.

If I am not busy and she happens to be free too, she takes me into her psychology department, where we can talk. There we are, all by ourselves in a little room containing a very narrow couch with a chair behind it, used for psychoanalytical sessions. P makes me lie down and takes the seat behind me. She can watch me, while I look at the wall opposite me

99

(which I do not mind). Just as if I were a patient. Except that she does all the talking and I only listen.

Sometimes I do not even listen. I just muse. I have become so used to her chatter that it does not disturb my own train of thought.

Today P is cross with me because I turned down her suggestion that we should meet in the psychology room. I said I wanted to listen to the 'Know Other Levels' talk. I did not mean to annoy her, but for once I wanted to have my own way, because these talks interest me. They bring something new into my life each day.

MAY 18

Levels 5, 4 and 3 form a group quite distinct from the military group of Levels 7 and 6. They are all civilian levels. But this is not the only thing they have in common. All three are set aside for the *élite* of the civilian society. And the more important the civilian, the deeper he will descend and the safer he will be.

Level 5 is reserved for 20,000 of the country's top citizens, the real pick of society. It consists of four independent units, in different parts of the country, and each unit will shelter 5,000 people at a depth of 1,500 feet. Their population will consist of top administrators, scientists, politicians, ex-generals (who count as civilians now) and their families.

Of course, there have to be a few technical experts on Level 5 too, people who do not rank high in society but are there simply to help run the place. In principle, however, the top *élite* is to look after itself with as little help from outsiders as possible. I dare say they will be willing enough to accept this when the only alternative is for Level 5 to hold less of them.

Each of the Level 5 units is located near one of the country's administrative or scientific centres, so that, when the moment comes, the privileged among its inhabitants can reach their shelter in time. Once down, they will not need to draw on the surface for any of their needs, for Level 5 is self-sufficient. They will not be quite so well off as we are in this respect, though: there will be relatively fewer auxiliary experts to help them along—less doctors and nurses, for example, even though they may have greater need of them. Still, the space is precious, and one more expert means one less VIP. Teachers and children's nurses will not be provided either, and for some reason I like to think of the *élite* having to do these jobs themselves. They will also need to learn how to handle sewage, keep the place clean, and so forth. It may be hard on them, but it will keep them busy.

Apart from that, they will have the same services that we enjoy on the military levels. Air and food will be supplied in the same way. So will energy, but not for such a long time: their supply is calculated to last for 200 years only.

MAY 19

Today X-107 and I discussed the advantages which the two military levels have over Level 5. He seems to derive some satisfaction from the fact that, judging by our lower level, we are rated as more important than our country's *élite*.

"Of course," he said, "this doesn't mean we'd have been above all those politicians and ex-generals and so on if all of us had stayed on the surface. But our military function makes it necessary for us to be given the most privileged position down here. The final victory—which means their welfare as well as ours—depends on us."

What X-107 had said made me think of the position of the captain on a big liner. Though some of his passengers may be eminent scientists or important statesmen, men of far more consequence, it is the captain who usually has the best-situated cabin. Of course, the importance of Level 7, or even

Level 6, relative to Level 5 is far greater than that of a captain to his passengers.

"I imagine," I said, "that the people of Level 5—who include our policy-makers, after all—would have put themselves on Levels 6 and 7 and us on Level 5 if there had been enough room for them down here. But they must have decided that getting a large number of themselves sheltered on a fairly deep level was better than having too few of them on Levels 6 and 7."

X-107 thought not. He said that whatever size the various levels had been, we should still have been allocated space on the deepest one because of our job.

Well, for one reason or another, the armed forces now find themselves in the safest place in the world, not in the front lines. Quite a change from the days when a soldier had to advance into a machine-gun volley and a pilot was forever expecting something to blast him out of the sky. Today we, the soldiers of our country, are shielded by an earth crust 3,000 or 4,400 feet thick. No warrior's armour-plating ever compared with that.

For once let the civilians tremble while the soldiers feel secure.

MAY 20

Levels 4 and 3 are designed on the same principle as Level 5. They have similar equipment and they are to house important people—though not so important as the *élite* of Level 5. The higher the level, once you get above the military units, the lower the social status of its prospective inhabitants.

Level 4 is sub-divided into ten independent and self-sufficient units, each holding 10,000 people. They are dispersed throughout the country, about 1,000 feet deep, and their food and energy supplies are planned to last about a century.

Level 3 is higher, about 500 feet deep, and has twenty-five units which will contain 20,000 persons each. So it will shelter in all half a million people. It has enough food and energy for about twenty-five years only.

The construction of Level 3 was in a way a harder task than that of Levels 4 and 5, simply because of the size of the units. Each must contain everything necessary for the life of 20,000 people, and though they will be more crowded and less convenient to live in than the units of Levels 4 and 5, not to mention Levels 6 and 7, the sheer magnitude of the building operation gave the designers some severe headaches.

Incidentally, the analogy of a ship was used by today's speaker, though rather differently from the way I used it. Levels 5, 4 and 3 correspond, according to him, to the first, second and third classes on a boat. Each is bigger than the preceding one and accommodates more passengers; and it is not quite as comfortable or well equipped.

I am sure the speaker was understating the facts. If he had to use a naval analogy, it would have been nearer the mark to compare Level 5 to the cheapest third-class berths, Level 4 to the deck of an immigrant ship, and Level 3 to the hold of a cattle boat or one of those hulks sailed by the old slave-traders. To start with first class was ridiculous. Even we Level 7 personnel are no more comfortable, by and large, than tourist-class passengers on a not very luxurious ship.

Besides, the analogy breaks down, as most analogies seem to below ground, unless you turn one half of it on its head. Whoever heard of a ship with the very best cabins at the bottom of the hold?

MAY 21

The talks about the different levels still hold their fascination for me. P cannot understand why, and it is useless trying to discuss such things with her. X-107 is the right sort of person for that—he always has been—and I am really lucky to have him as my room-mate.

The talks have tended to dwell on the differences between Levels 5, 4 and 3, which makes one forget that, in a sense, they form one very distinct group. I was reminded of the fact by X-107, who pointed out not only the similarity of their equipment and facilities, but also their basic social unity. "Despite the distinctions you may make between the *élite* of 20,000, the group of 100,000 and the mass of half a million people," he said, "they add up to only 620,000. This sounds a lot if you think of the difficulty of housing them all underground, but very few if you remember the size of the nation."

He was perfectly right. With a nine-figure population to take into consideration, 620,000 is a mere drop in the bucket.

"So," he went on, "to be picked for these levels is a real privilege. To be included in Levels 3 and 4, let alone Level 5, you'd have to belong to the pick of society—or else be married to the right person or have the right parents. Then if people are going to bring their families down with them, I suppose they'll want to stay together and live something like a normal civilian life." X-107 shook his head doubtfully. "That's not nearly as orderly and rational as our system. I'm sure there will be awful complications."

I smiled at his seriousness and said, with some mischief: "But what will an *élite* do when it's all on its own. If an *élite* hasn't a crowd to contrast itself with, what will happen to it? I think living by themselves may prove hard for our select civilians—and not only the honoured few on Level 5."

X-107 thought this might indeed be an interesting sociological problem. He suggested that, under the pressure of seclusion, each group would develop new fine grades of social distinction within itself, so that before long each underground unit would form a little social pyramid of its own.

I found this idea fascinating. "Who do you think would come out on the very top in a cave of, say, 5,000 top people?" I asked. "It couldn't be the statesmen, because down here there won't be much in the way of international politics."

X-107 disagreed: he thought that international matters could be negotiated from the caves by means of radio.

"Even if that's so," I retorted, "they won't have so much *national* politics to talk about. There will surely be very little going on in the international sphere after an atomic war. Radioactivity will keep everybody below ground for a long time, and they won't have a chance to build more atomic rockets to replace the ones we've fired. No more rockets, no more wars. There will be no point in making alliances either. No alliances, no wars—politics won't be politics any more."

"There's still something else they can do," X-107 replied a little wistfully. "They can abuse each other over the radio."

"If they're not too busy washing their grandchildren's diapers," I added.

This made X-107 laugh. "Maybe this will be the new social yardstick on the civilian levels," he said. "The person who proves to be most useful, best adjusted, cleverest at improvising things and solving day-to-day problems—he'll rise in status. The rest will go down."

"Not down," I replied jokingly. "To be down is the greatest privilege. Look at us!"

MAY 22

Today P persuaded me to join her again in the little room in the psychology department, as we both happened to be free at the same time. I was not eager to go, but I could think of no excuse on the spur of the moment and so I agreed.

I lay down on the couch as usual, while P took the chair behind me and started to chatter. I hardly listened and really had no idea what she was saying, for my mind was moving around Levels 5, 4 and 3.

I was wondering how closely the enemy's underground shelters resembled our own. The shelters for civilians, I mean.

There seemed little doubt that the deepest levels would be reserved for the push-button military forces, as ours were. Ways of life and ideologies might differ, but bottom-level priority for the armed forces was an obvious military necessity.

But how about the civilian levels? What were the differences there? It seemed to me again that the enemy's arrangements were probably very much like ours: who was more likely to be on their lowest civilian level than the politicians, administrators and retired generals? As for the other levels, there might be the difference that in one country the rich got the better shelter, and in another country the mighty.

But was this really such a big difference? I wondered. The rich were mighty and the mighty were rich. And atomic scientists and technicians and engineers fitted both categories: nowadays they were well-off and influential in any part of the world.

Taken all in all, I decided, whatever the differences in ideology on the *surface,* the *inside* might look very similar. (I mean the surface and the inside of the earth, of course. Or do I?)

I became aware that P was trying to get me to answer a question. She repeated it several times until I grasped it: "Which do you like best, our official privacy room or this one?"

Still only half with her, I answered: "Oh, they look much the same."

MAY 23

The 'Know Other Levels' talks have reached Levels 2 and 1. These form another group, distinct not only from the military levels but also from 5, 4 and 3. They are to house ordinary civilians, not an *élite.* Eventually there will be enough shelters on these levels for everybody, but that goal is still some way off.

The technical arrangements on Levels 2 and 1 are different from those on all the previous levels.

To begin with, fresh air will be drawn down from the surface, not supplied by plants. It will pass through filters, of course, but how effective they will be in the event of a full-scale atomic war remains to be seen. Even the speaker did not sound too optimistic about that. "To supply so many people with air by means of plants was technically impossible—certainly in the time at our disposal," he said. "It will be a stupendous achievement if, by the time the war starts, the entire population has been provided with shelters of *any* sort."

The energy for Levels 2 and 1 is supplied by conventional generators and not by atomic reactors, which are too few to go round and which would have to be supervised by experts. The conventional generators, which are much easier for non-specialists to handle, will be fed by pipes from fuel reservoirs. Some of these are underground, but most of them are on the surface. In the event of a near hit the latter sort will be destroyed, and then the dependent shelter, even if not damaged itself, will be in a fix. But this cannot be helped.

Food for the top levels will be supplied just as it is lower down. But there will not be much of it: enough for six months on Level 2 and only enough for one month on Level 1.

"This may surprise you," the speaker said, "but I think you will see how pointless it would be to make provision for longer periods—even if the storage space were available. Levels 2 and 1 are too close to the surface to resist an all-out enemy attack: 100 feet deep in the case of Level 2, and ten to sixty feet deep in the other. They may perhaps survive blast effects, provided the enemy uses no thermonuclear bombs of the underground-bursting type. If the war should be conducted in such a limited fashion, and if there is no excessive residual radiation, then after a month or so people may be able to go back to the surface without disastrous results. But if *total* war is waged, there will be so much physical destruction and air pollution that most living creatures so near the surface will not be able to survive. Possibly some of the Level 2 units, or even Level 1, will be lucky, if they are far enough away from an underground explosion. But this is not at all likely."

The outlook seems grim; but one must agree that there is little point in giving shelters enough provisions to last for years if they are not physically strong enough to withstand the explosion of an underground-bursting multi-megaton bomb.

It is clear that people on these levels stand a very slim chance of surviving unless the war is a fairly limited one. But it is not likely to be. It strikes me that Levels 2 and 1 must have been built more for their psychological effect than for any other reason. They will mislead the safety-seeking masses into supposing they can find it from ten to a hundred feet underground!

MAY 24

Level 2 has room for about one million people. It is subdivided into forty units holding 25,000 each.

The social composition of its future inhabitants is peculiarly interesting. This level is destined to receive all kinds of maladjusted people: peace-mongers, extreme oppositionists, critics of society and other cranks.

"The idea behind this," said the speaker today, "is to appease all the doubtful and subversive elements by giving them a more secure and privileged shelter level. It is better to adopt these measures than to resort to sheer force alone."

The 'alone' was significant, I thought. I do not know how much force has been, or will be, necessary; but there are plenty of legal restrictions to protect the atomic means of protection from the assaults of all sorts of sceptics. These people must have been mollified by the promise of a deeper shelter. I say 'must have been' because I am guessing. I have no way of knowing what the effect actually was, because when I was up on the surface nobody knew about the seven levels. We knew that shelters were being built all over the country—that fact could hardly be hidden—but nobody even suggested that they might possibly be on different levels.

So the peace-mongers and other assorted cranks are fortunate to be booked for Level 2 and not Level 1.

In theory, anyway. In practice the difference will be negligible. Is a shelter 100 feet deep any use against a multimegaton bomb which explodes underground to produce an effect like an earthquake? Even supposing such a shelter is far enough away from the burst to be safe, half a year's provisions will only prolong life for a little while: the surface may be polluted for many years—the fall-out of underground bursts would be specially dangerous, not to speak of the 'rigged' bombs—and the only alternatives will be to die of starvation underground or be killed by radiation on top.

Even so, they may regard themselves as very privileged at the present moment, for the mass of the population has shelters closer to the surface. Moreover, half the population still has no shelters at all! Construction is going on very fast, but even so it will be at least six months before there is room for everyone. Whether the war holds off that long is anybody's guess.

The shelters on Level 1 vary in size: some of them are designed to hold a million people, some as few as 10,000. One reason for this is the variation in density of population from one part of the country to another. Also, it has been necessary to exploit all existing underground space; which means that whereas one place may have big ready-made shelters in its underground transport system, another place may have to start from nothing and build smaller shelters where it can.

Hundreds have already been built up and down the country, and every day more are being finished.

But there is no point in talking about Level 1 at length, and that goes for Level 2 as well. Unless the war is a very limited one, they do not stand a chance.

MAY 25

P is rather worried about me. She thinks my preoccupation with the other levels is not good for me. I am enjoying this hobby too much, she says, and it may end in mental depression—the sort I have had before. (By now she knows a little more about me, because she is my wife—if I may call her that—or because she is a psychologist. Or maybe because she is both.)

She thinks my keen interest in other levels is a symptom of emotional instability. Today she was going on about different levels of consciousness, symbolism and what not. I really do not care. If something wants to take hold of my mind, I let it.

In any case, the 'Know Other Levels' series ended today with a talk about the preparations on the surface—Level 0, the speaker called it, and I suppose the term was convenient for his purpose, though of course the surface is not a real level at all.

Up there they have been getting everything organised for a general descent, which must take place quickly but smoothly and without fuss at a moment's notice. As the operation involves—in principle, at least—the entire population, its efficiency is of primary importance.

The speaker said that many people have already been issued identity badges bearing their names, levels and shelter numbers, which they wear pinned to their chests. The rest are anxiously awaiting their badges.

"There is some ill-feeling among people who assume that

segregation into different levels means social discrimination," said the speaker, "but it stays within reasonable bounds." Apparently people have a vague idea that Level 5 is better than Level 4, Level 4 better than Level 3, and so on; but they do not know exactly what the difference is. Most of them imagine it is a matter of convenience and luxury, not of safety. Up there the information we have been given in our daily talks is top secret.

Most of the hostility—and it is mixed with anxiety—comes from people who do not yet possess an identity badge and shelter number, which will act as a sort of passport to the underground. The hostility is directed, naturally enough, at those who have already been given their badges. This is tending to split the nation into two opposed groups—a new kind of division between the haves and the have-nots. However, the dangers of this ill-feeling are being mitigated by the fact that more and more people are receiving their badges ("and the right to be buried alive", I thought of adding). The moment they get them, they become the strongest supporters of the system.

It is only among the prospective inhabitants of Level 1 that this last trouble has arisen. All the people destined for the other levels have already got their passports. There are a few grumblers among the cranks and peace-mongers of Level 2, admittedly, but not many. The receipt of Level 2 badges has made even the most fervent critics a great deal less eloquent.

MAY 26

I miss the 'Know Other Levels' talks. No new talks programme has been announced so far. Probably because there is nothing to talk about. Now that we know Level 7 thoroughly and have a fair working knowledge of the other levels, what else can they find to discuss? Even with the diversity of seven levels, the amount of variety underground is very limited. It must be, just as the caves are.

I have been listening to music today. By now the tunes have become rather familiar.

It is an odd sensation, knowing so much about other levels, while the people up there know so little about the kind of life—if you can call this life—which is waiting for them. I feel like an omniscient being, severed from contact with other human beings, but knowing all about what is going to happen to them.

If God exists—in heaven, or in the centre of the earth—He must feel the same way. In seclusion He watches the impending disaster which is about to overtake the ant-like human beings. Watches with interest, but also with detachment.

But perhaps He envies them sometimes. There they are, all the ants, running about, enjoying each other's company, planning, analysing, discussing, believing, criticising. And there He is—alone. Wiser, more powerful, but alone.

I wonder if sometimes He would like to change places: to be miserably weak, but to have company and so many interests. They may be petty interests, stupid ones; but they keep the mind busy.

Maybe this is the reason why gods—the Greek ones, at least —used sometimes to descend to earth and mix with men. They must have become bored with their own company.

MAY 27

Today it got me again.

It had been an ordinary routine day, nothing unusual, until sometime between 17.00 and 18.00 hours, when I suddenly saw the green fields near my native town. I knew perfectly well that it was my imagination, but the whole scene was sharp and bright in front of my eyes.

I do not know why it happened. It may have had something to do with the good violet perfume used by the nurse sitting next to me at lunch—she must have brought it down with her. I remember thinking how nice it smelled. Then I must have forgotten it until several hours later, when the memory brought with it the image of the meadows.

Different shades of green grass: some dark, some light and fresh. Trees and hills and the cool breeze of a spring afternoon. Blue skies with bright clouds. And people scattered here and there, and twittering birds. And a deep peace of mind, a feeling that I was alive and that being alive was enough. No need to do anything, or achieve anything, or struggle for anything. And deep breathing to welcome all the sweet scents of soil and grass and spring flowers into my breast.

No, it's no use trying. It takes a poet to convey sensations like those. I have never been one, and poets do not grow in caves. But today, I think, I felt the way poets must feel. The vision was so sharp, so powerful, that for a moment I forgot where I was.

Was it for just a moment? I have no way of telling, for I have lost all sense of time.

But then the image disappeared, and in its place came longing for those meadows and those days. It came like a sharp pain, throbbing with increasing vigour, until I wanted to cry out and bang my head against the clean, hygienic, sterile walls.

I did nothing. Gradually the pangs subsided. But despair filled my mind, despair as black as those fields were green, as bitter as that spring breeze was sweet. There is no need for poetry to convey that.

P said today that she knew this was going to happen to me and that she had warned me. It is too late now, anyway.

I am so depressed that I do not want to do anything—except one thing: to get back to the surface. If I could do that I would willingly give up Level 7 for Level 1. Indeed, I would not care if they allotted me no level at all! Even if it meant spending just a very short time up above, just a day. To live for a day, and then perish!

Butterflies live for only a day, but they do *live*. Not in caves, but in the full light of the sun. Among flowers. They fly around from one blossom to another, in whatever direction they like.

I suppose complaining will not do any good, but what else *can* I do? Eat, meet P, talk with X-107 and sleep. That is the sum of my 'activities'.

I can push the buttons, of course—when somebody decides it is necessary. That is an activity, certainly. But is it enough?

No, much too simple. Why did they make it so easy? Just pushing a few buttons—where is the fun in that?

And what next? What do I do when I have pushed my buttons? What will there be left for me when I have fulfilled my life's function? What other goal shall I look forward to?

Shall I be like God before He created the world, sitting lonely in an empty universe? How cruel men were to create a God who is self-sufficient living a solitary life throughout eternity. Why have they condemned God, why have they condemned me, to such a lonely prison?

P tries hard to help me. She really is anxious about my present mood. She has even encouraged me to resume the conversations about mythology which I used to enjoy with R-747. She says that would be better than brooding all the time.

But I do not feel like it. Why should I? Do gods invent mythology for people? Let the future generations invent what stories they like. I do not care what they think.

X-107's attempts to make me talk about things do not succeed any more, either. Nothing interests me any more. Nothing down here, at least.

P is in despair about me. She must like me very much. Apparently she is quite sociable, after all. She is doing her best to drag me out of my apathy.

I see her point quite well, but I cannot be bothered to make the effort. Why should I?

Does this mean I have become self-sufficient? I want nothing of anybody or anything down here. Perhaps that makes me the most self-sufficient creature on Level 7. Like a god!

Maybe I *am* a god, or about to become a god! Let R-747 invent myths about me, the god who pushed the buttons. X-127, the push-button god.

No, I have not pushed the buttons yet. But I *am* self-sufficient like a god. Not as happy, though. Not even as happy as the butterfly which is born and dies on the same day. But who said that gods should be happy?

I am a god. The god wants to make a bargain with a butterfly. He wishes to be a butterfly for a day—but outside the caves, up there—and he offers the butterfly in return an eternal existence—down here.

What do you say to that, butterfly? Will you agree to the bargain? It's a good one: eternity for one day of flying among the flowers.

The butterfly rejects my offer. What is it saying?

It says it will not exchange one day of happiness for eternal misery! Damnable butterfly! The audacity to refuse a god's bargain! To defy a god! To defy God!

I shall curse you, butterfly, you colourful hedonist, I shall curse you till the end of your days!

It says something. It dares to answer! What is it?

"I do not mind your curses, O God, for my day is short." It flies away.

Butterfly! Butterfly! Listen to me, don't go away! Stay with me, I won't curse you. But stay here with me. Wait! Please stay!

JUNE 7

Today I came back from the psychological department. I spent about a week there.

Apparently I was going mad. Quite raving, as I can see for myself from what I was writing on May 31. All that nonsense about gods and butterflies! It seems I even got my entomology wrong: butterflies, so P told me when I had finished muttering about them under the drug, live for longer than a day. Some even hibernate!

Anyway, I am all right now. Only weak and tired and empty, as if someone has removed my inside. Metaphorically, that is. My mind and soul feel empty, just as if they had been purged in the way my stomach was, after the wedding chocolate.

It is a good thing, this mental purge. I do not suffer now.

Nor do I enjoy my awareness of things. I just am and do not mind being.

I still have the memory of something being wrong with me, but the thing itself has gone away. It was a more complicated business than the stomach purge, though. They had to give me drugs and some electric shock treatment to clean out my mind. But now I am quiet and all right.

JUNE 9

It happened this morning.

I started my spell of duty in the PBX Operations Room at 08.00 hours. At 09.00 the yellow light came on above the screen. Two minutes later X-117 walked into the room and took his place at the other table, ready for whatever might follow the yellow warning. The Operations Room was now prepared for action. We sat in silence, watching the light.

At 09.12 hours the functional loudspeaker in the room suddenly ordered: "Attention! Prepare for action!" Simultaneously, the yellow light was replaced by a red one.

The loudspeaker spoke again: "Push Button A1!"

I pressed the button, and X-117 must have pushed his too, for Zone A on the screen suddenly became covered with red points. This meant that the one-to-five megaton rockets had been released and were now flying with incredible speed towards their targets. Zone A being relatively near, the results were to be expected in less than half an hour.

I was sitting in my place watching the screen. I was more tense than usual, but I did not feel nervous. Perhaps because of the treatment I underwent last week. Perhaps because military action—for the first time I was doing what I had come down here to do—acted as a sort of relief.

I glanced across the room at X-117, and I thought he looked very much on edge. Though the room was at a com-

117

fortable temperature, his face was sweating profusely, as if he had been pushing not a button but the rockets themselves.

Then I turned my eyes back to the screen, and sat speculating as to whether it would all amount to no more than an exchange of smallish bombs limited to one area, or whether the operation would develop into full-scale hostilities.

At 09.32 hours the first rocket hit enemy territory and one of the red spots turned into a rather larger circular red blob. Almost at once more such blobs appeared here and there over Zone A. I saw how the area of destruction grew wider and wider.

Meanwhile, though, some of the little red spots were disappearing, particularly the ones deeper in Zone A. Apparently the enemy's interceptors were quite efficient.

Then, at 09.55, the loudspeaker sounded again: "Attention! Push Button A2!" And immediately afterwards: "Push Button A3!"

I reacted quickly, and so did X-117, and the loudspeaker had hardly finished before Zone A became covered with a mass of blue and golden points.

Æsthetically the picture was quite pleasing. Red blobs and blue and yellow spots, some on the red blobs and some outside them. But the colour was still restricted to Zone A. The other zones remained white, like a continent waiting for an explorer to map it.

I wondered what impression the news would make on P. Also on other people who would meet me in the lounge and ask me about it all. I thought about this, that and the other —like during a concert, when one's thoughts wander far away from the music.

.   .   .   .   .

At 10.10 came the next order from the loudspeaker: "Push Button B1, push Button B2, push Button B3, push Button C1!"

We pushed four times. Now all the map was unevenly spotted with points in three colours.

Five minutes later the blue and yellow spots in Zone A started to change into circular blots. The blue ones were particularly big: these indicated the destruction resulting from the blast and heat of multi-megaton bombs which were bursting in the air to cause very widespread damage. Areas ranging from hundreds to thousands of square miles were being wiped out.

It was obvious from the screen that this bombing was proving much more effective than the first lot. Perhaps the enemy was running short of interceptors, or else our A2 and A3 missiles were fitted with some anti-interceptor device which the A1 rockets did not possess. Whatever the explanation, the blue and golden circles were steadily obliterating Zone A, and soon the red circles looked almost insignificant. There were very few of them which were not surrounded by circles of yellow or blue. The blue was steadily spreading over the zone, with smaller golden and red blobs superimposed like stars in a night sky.

At 10.40 the dots in Zone B started their metamorphosis into circles. This time the process was different, for red, blue and yellow circles appeared simultaneously. They were all there competing for space.

The coloured 'exploration' progressed into the heart of Zone B almost unchecked. Apparently there were no more obstacles in the way of our missiles. The 'terra incognita' of the map was rapidly becoming nicely tinted. It looked as though the final picture would be much like that in Zone A, with blue covering most of the ground and yellow and red superimposed on it in smaller areas.

．　　　．　　　．　　　．　　　．

The spots started to spread in Zone C at 10.55. This time there were only red ones, so the process could be seen more clearly.

119

But there appeared to be some trouble, for a large number of the spots disappeared, meaning that the missiles had not found their marks. Either the enemy had some defensive counter-measures in Zone C, or else our rockets were simply failing to reach there. Perhaps it was the greater range that was the difficulty. Certainly something had gone wrong.

At 11.00 hours we received another order, from a different voice this time: "Press Button C2, press Button C3!"

We pushed and waited again.

There were only three buttons left unpushed—the supposedly most dangerous ones, which controlled the batteries of 'rigged' bombs. Their radioactivity would make the areas they hit uninhabitable not just in the immediate future but for years to come. Perhaps for generations.

It had always been doubted whether these bombs would be used at all, for in all probability their effect would not be limited to the territory directly hit but would also spread to neighbouring countries. And there were no grounds for annihilating neutrals. Even more to the point, these bombs might endanger our own existence. No country wants a suicidal war!

"Or does it?" I began to ask myself; but the thought was quickly banished from my mind by the loudspeaker (in its original voice): "Attention! Push Button A4, push Button B4, push Button C4!"

I glanced at the clock—11.15 hours—and pressed the three buttons. Then I looked up at the map, and was puzzled to find that no black marks had appeared. I pushed the buttons again. Nothing happened.

Then the loudspeaker—it was voice number two again—practically shouted: "Officer X-117! Push Buttons A4! B4! C4!"

I turned and looked at X-117. He was sitting in his chair staring at the buttons, while his arms hung limply as if someone had severed the nerves. He did not stir, but there were some sounds coming from his lips.

They were hardly audible, but after a while I could make out what he was saying: "No! Anything but those! Not Buttons 4! I can't kill my mother! No, not those . . ."

The Operations Room door suddenly swung open and two men—from the medical department, I think—dragged X-117 from the room. His arms were still hanging limply, and as he staggered out of the doorway he went on repeating: "No! Not Buttons 4. . . ."

I had no time to reflect on what had happened. X-107 entered the room and quietly took X-117's place at the other table. X-137 came in behind him—apparently to replace me if necessary.

The loudspeaker sounded again (by now the time was 11.20): "Push Button A4, push Button B4, push Button C4!"

This time it went without a hitch.

At 11.21 hours today the 9th of June, I was through with my daily duty. As a matter of fact, I was through with my life's work. I had done my job. My function as PBX Officer was completely fulfilled.

The loudspeaker said: "You are free, gentlemen. You may go to your quarters or, if you prefer, stay to watch the results of A4, B4 and C4."

X-107 and X-137 remained behind to see what happened. I came back here to my room and lay down.

JUNE 10

So the war is over. It started yesterday at 09.12 hours, as far as our offensive action was concerned, and it ended when our last missiles exploded in enemy territory at 12.10 hours.

The whole war lasted two hours and fifty-eight minutes—the shortest war in history. And the most devastating one. For both these reasons it is very easy to write its history: no complicated and lengthy campaigns, no battlefields to remember —the globe was one battlefield.

I could summarise this war, the greatest in human history, in a few words: "Yesterday, in a little under three hours, life on vast patches of the earth was annihilated." But I had better be more historically minded and write down a few details about how it happened. These details were announced on the general loudspeaker system first thing this morning, and have been repeated several times since. Everybody knows them now almost by heart. I shall reproduce them true to their spirit, even if the wording differs a little from the original.

Yesterday, at 09.07 hours, twelve H-bombs fell in a remote part of our country. Ten of them exploded in sparsely inhabited areas, but two hit big centres of population. The attack came suddenly, and by the time PBY Command detected the missiles they were already striking their targets. No interception of these rockets was possible, but their arrival served as the best possible warning and PBY Command's later achievements were spectacular.

But PBX Command too was alive to what was going on. The treacherous attack had to be met with a counter-attack, and so the command "Push Button A1" was given. The command was limited, quite conscientiously, to just the one button. We did not want to start a total war as long as we were not sure that the enemy intended to annihilate us completely. Button A1 released only two thousand rockets, with warheads of one to five megatons. They were directed solely at military and industrial installations in the nearest enemy zone.

At the same time, in case the enemy should retaliate, the alarm was sounded throughout the country and people hurried underground. This was done in a fairly orderly manner, except for some trouble over the Level 1 shelters. Many people without the proper identification tried to get into them, and this led to rioting. It is likely that many people who should not have gone below did so, while some who were entitled to a place were left outside. The shelters became overcrowded, and in the struggle for space many women, children and old people were crushed to death. These scenes went on for as long as the areas concerned were not hit; and the longer they were spared the bombs, the worse the fighting became. In some places it was over in forty minutes or so, but here and there it lasted up to two hours, with bloody battles which became even more ferocious as distant explosions were heard. Entrances to shelters were blocked by people fighting in the most primitive and cruel way with the nearest weapons that came to hand—kitchen knives, clubs made from broken-up furniture, and bare fists if they could not find anything better. All this was reported over the radio by self-sacrificing commentators, who even in this emergency did not forget their duty to report the news. They died, microphones in hand.

At 09.15 hours, three minutes after our first operational move, our leaders received a radio message from the enemy which announced that twelve intercontinental missiles with H-bomb warheads had escaped their electronic controls and might explode in our country. The message asked us not to retaliate, as this was not an intentional act of hostility but only a technical accident.

We replied that we should have been warned earlier so that we could intercept the missiles as successfully as possible.

The enemy answered that it had taken them some time to realise what had happened, and even longer to get in touch with us.

This sounded very suspicious. We had to be on guard, of course, against a treacherous attempt by the enemy to test our vulnerability by sending a sample of twelve rockets with the excuse that they had 'escaped' their controls. So we did not give any details about the explosions in our country (though the enemy must have got the general picture on whatever corresponds over there to our PBX viewing screen); nor did we tell the enemy about the two thousand rockets which were already on their way and would shortly be touching ground and exploding in his Zone A. We just went on arguing about the enemy's twelve bombs until 09.32 hours, when our rockets started arriving. As results have shown, the enemy was taken quite as much by surprise as we had been. The difference was that he had surprised us with twelve bombs; we surprised him with two thousand.

Then we waited. We hoped the enemy would interpret this limited counter-attack on a limited area as a warning—a warning in action, to be sure, not in words.

Unfortunately his viciousness was beyond reasoning with. For, on being hit by our rockets, he immediately released a huge quantity of his own, thousands of multi-megaton missiles, against our country and our allies. These started exploding at 09.50 in the areas nearest to his rocket bases, and gradually reached deeper and deeper into our territory.

Meanwhile we did not sit doing nothing, of course. PBY Command was ready for the attack this time, and automatically controlled interceptors destroyed hundreds of enemy missiles even before they reached this country, mostly over allied territories. But many more hundreds—thousands, to be exact—exploded at their predestined targets.

Naturally, as the enemy's attack spread, our offensive branch retaliated powerfully. Thousands of missiles were fired into the remotest corners of the enemy's country and those of his satellites, spreading death and annihilation.

One other critical moment occurred when, at 11.15 hours, our gadgets discovered that the enemy had started using rigged bombs—the highly radioactive ones. This was the most barbaric thing to do, but we had long ago realised to what atrocious extremes the enemy was likely to go. We were ready for this too, and we hit back.

We hit hard. Thousands of our missiles fitted with H-bombs in highly radioactive shells were sent to hit the enemy and his

124

satellites wherever they might have survived. This happened at 11.20 and was our last act of war.

The last of our bombs exploded at 12.10 hours. The enemy's last bomb had hit us at 11.45. Presumably he had run out of missiles, or had had all his launching sites destroyed, even before our rigged bombs arrived to have the last word in the argument.

Needless to say, we are the victors.

JUNE 11

There is radio contact between ourselves and the enemy—between the two undergrounds, that is. Though the bombs have had their decisive say in the main argument, a kind of quarrelling post-mortem is being carried on by the spoken word. And all today the general loudspeaker system has been relaying these verbal exchanges.

This morning the enemy accused us of starting this disastrous war. He maintained that the twelve rockets which hit us in the first place were just an accident, the outcome of a technical failure, and that to retaliate with two thousand bombs was a war crime of the worst sort.

We answered that, if he had had no intention of making war on us, he should not have answered our first bombing with a much more violent attack of his own. He should have refrained from action.

The enemy replied that the launching of two thousand H-bombs was not an action he could very well ignore. And retaliation, in order to be effective, always had to be more powerful than the act which provoked it.

The argument went on in this fashion for some time, each side trying to shift the blame on to the shoulders of the other.

"It is your leaders," shouted the enemy's spokesman, "who will be condemned by future generations and by history for giving that order to launch two thousand rockets in response to a mere technical mishap."

Our reply to this accusation startled me. The speaker retorted: "Our leaders did not give the order! It was given automatically when your twelve H-bombs exploded in our country!"

He went on to explain that for safety's sake we had not relied entirely on our leaders, who, being human, were subject to human weakness and fallibility and could be sick, meet with accidents and what not. Certainly they *could* have given an order to attack, but in fact they did *not* issue such an order. It was done by a mysterious gadget called an 'atomphone'.

This was an intricate and ingenious device which was said to be sensitive to atomic explosions occurring within a limited range: it would react to an explosion in our country, but not one in enemy territory. Though the atomphone utilised the principle of the seismograph, its function depended also on its sensitivity to acoustic waves, electro-magnetic radiation and some other properties. Thus it would *not* react to a mere earthquake. Moreover, it could classify the strength of the explosion. Once the atomphone had registered an atomic explosion, it would automatically issue the order for retaliation of the appropriate strength.

The twelve exploding H-bombs made this gadget set in motion the minimum retaliatory attack. Thus the first two thousand rockets were released.

This certainly *was* interesting news. Our politicians must have been still on the way to their shelters on Level 5 when the actual command was taken over by the atomphone. And this device issued the order heard by X-117 and myself, "Push Button A1," which was probably tape-recorded.

The enemy's reply to this news was surprisingly similar. Their leaders too did not actually give any instructions to strike back. As with us, any attack automatically set off a counter-attack of greater strength.

So the picture of what really happened starts to become clear. In all probability the war *did* start by accident. The retaliation *was* automatic. So was the retaliation to the retaliation, and so on. (The only exceptions, on our side, were the command to push Buttons C2 and C3, given locally on Level 7 because the C1 bombing was not quite effective, and the repeated command to push A4, B4 and C4, which had to be given locally because of X-117's breakdown. And this explains why the voice giving the orders changed twice.) As each retaliatory measure was automatically more powerful than the attack which caused it, it was inevitable that the war should develop with increasing violence until the arsenal of one side was completely exhausted. As it happened, the two sides were of roughly equal strength and at the end *neither* side had anything left to fire.

Thus the progress of the war resembled the chain reaction going on inside the atomic bomb itself! On the other hand, it followed the pattern of most of the wars in history. One difference, and a big one, was that it was a war of weapons which fought by themselves, not of human beings armed with weapons.

I wonder why they needed to have PBX Command. The atomphones could have released the rockets directly, instead of ordering human beings to do it. What was the point of using *us*?

I suppose our leaders might have decided to attack on their own initiative, and then they would have needed us to carry out their orders. Or it might have happened that, in retaliation for a provocative attack, they would decide to use all our power at once. Such a decision could not have been made automatically. (Just think! If all the buttons had been pushed together, the war would have been over in about an hour.)

As it turned out, this was nearly as automatic a war as could be imagined. PBX Command was the only human link in the battle of gadgets. For that reason, as X-107 once correctly reasoned, we had to be housed in a safe place inside the earth.

It looks as if all that talk yesterday about our 'hope' and the enemy's 'viciousness' was just so much old-fashioned propaganda. The human decisions were made long in advance. Then the gadgets took over and ordered the operational moves when the actual situation corresponded with the hypothetical one in the minds of the planners.

Perhaps the whole thing would never have happened if those twelve enemy rockets had not escaped their controls. It was just an accident, a sort of joke played on us all by—well, I do not know whose joke it was. The gods? Fortune? The devil? It really does not matter. It is all over now. The gadgets have destroyed themselves, and the buttons in the PBX Operations Room can become playthings for children.

No doubt something has changed, though. Up there the scene must have changed completely. Who has survived? Which levels go on existing? How many people have become the victims of this war of gadgets? Has humanity been destroyed by its own ingenuity?

These questions do not sound quite real, for down here on Level 7 everything is just as it was, except that I have no more work to do. But still . . . it will be interesting to find out how much of our country is left.

JUNE 12

The Operations Room has become a sort of museum. Or a sanctuary, if you like. Where once Security forbade any but my brother button-pushers and me to tread, anybody may now wander around.

I visited the place again today, for the first time since our operations. People keep drifting in to look around the room and play with the 'keys' of the 'typewriters'. Some of them asked me some pretty silly questions.

"Was pushing the buttons a very difficult thing to do?" enquired one woman. I laughed and told her that it was the simplest job imaginable. A child could have done it. An imbecile. A trained monkey!

My answer to the woman's enquiry provoked a question in my own mind: Why did I have such a long and intensive training? Was it really necessary? Or was it really *training?* What skill had I acquired? Enough to push the buttons! And I had learnt all sorts of technical things seemingly unrelated to this imbecile function. My guess was that the training staff introduced them to make me feel that I had an intricate and important job to do, and to camouflage the simplicity of my basic task. This sort of 'training' must have been the crafty invention of my wife's colleagues—psychologists. They studied monkeys to learn about men, and then turned men into monkeys.

While I was brooding over this, someone called my attention to the screen. I wonder why I did not look at it as soon as I entered the room.

It was in its usual place, where I had seen it every day since coming down here. But when I left it at 11.21 hours on June 9, the enemy's territory was covered with rather nicely-coloured spots and circles. Now it was completely black.

A4, B4 and C4 had done a thorough job. They had added over-all radioactive poisoning to the blast and heat damage. Not an acre of ground belonging to the enemy or anybody on his side had escaped. Not a single coloured spot, let alone white, was left.

It gave me a curious chilly feeling. Not so much the destruction, as the completeness of it. This may have been quite irrational; but the unrelieved black made me turn and leave the Operations Room hurriedly, determined not to go back there again.

I wonder how *our* map looks, down there in the enemy's ex-X Operations Room. Are there still some coloured places on it—red, blue, yellow—even some white parts? Or is it all black?

At last—some news about the destruction outside.

It appears to be total. As complete as that over territory held by the enemy, if one can go by the message they broadcast today: that their 'Offensive Actions Operations Room' screen showed our country, and those of our allies, lying in ruins.

As far as anybody can ascertain, no one is still living on the surface of our country. Not one radio message has been received. Of course, nobody is going to peep out and check the situation just at the moment. The radioactivity would be fatal.

Moreover, there is no radio contact with any shelter on Level 1, though each of these was equipped with a short-wave transmitter and receiver. We have called them, but not a squeak has been got out of them so far. They must all have been destroyed by the underground-bursting bombs—though some were probably hit by the ground-bursting and even the air-bursting ones as well.

But what difference does it make how they perished? They perished.

It looks as if all our allies have suffered the same fate. Judging by the complete radio silence, they have been wiped out not only on the surface but even in their shelters; which is not all that surprising, since the shelters were of a rather primitive and inefficient sort. The Level 1 type.

This means that only a very small percentage of our population survived the war. And the same goes, of course, for our enemy. (His satellites were no luckier than our allies.)

The world is no longer over-populated. Hundreds of millions died in those three hours. Hundreds of millions in three hours!

There is full radio contact with Levels 6, 5, 4 and 3. The

military levels and those of the civilian *élite* were deep enough to survive the terrible blast. The civilians—especially the VIPs—must be having a hard time, getting adjusted to the underground life they entered so suddenly, but they can count themselves fortunate to be alive at all.

The lot of Level 2 is perhaps the most interesting of all, because this level has proved to be just on the border of survival. Of the forty shelters, thirty-two were too near to underground explosions to survive. But eight shelters, with about 25,000 people in each, are intact. We have radio links with them.

I cannot think why, but they keep asking us for details about what is happening on the surface. Even after they have been given the correct answer (which boils down to 'Nothing'), they go on asking such pointless questions as, for example, "Why weren't better shelters built for more people?" As if anything can be done about it now!

It seems that under stress they are becoming more critical again. Some of them have been making abusive remarks about our government—accusing it of 'negligence', 'stupidity' and so forth.

It is good fun listening to these messages. They have real entertainment value.

That is one of the best things about these post-war days—the radio communication. For the first time since we came down here, we can hear the voice of people outside our own community. Not voices from the surface, admittedly, but voices from other levels. We communicate with the other military people on Level 6, we overhear what the politicians say on Level 5, we enjoy ourselves listening to the abuse from the cranks who survive on Level 2.

And all quite unrestricted, too. Since June 11 the general loudspeaker system has been relaying whatever messages have seemed of most general interest. As far as I can tell, the selection necessary in the circumstances (the alternative would be babel) is the only form of 'censorship' being used.

There cannot be any other kind, or we should certainly not be allowed to hear the outrageous things said by the enemy and by Level 2.

Level 7, it seems to me, has been reborn. People are taking an interest in what is going on in the world—or rather in the underworld. There is a new sparkle in their eyes.

We are no longer isolated. We have contact with humanity again.

We are not underprivileged any more, doomed to live below while others enjoy the sunshine. Now we appreciate how privileged we are. Our deepest of shelters makes us the most favoured people in the world.

JUNE 14

P is very satisfied with my present mental condition. I am in a much better mood, and have almost forgotten the ordeal of my psychological therapy.

The activity, the feeling of having done something, does me good. I am through with my work now, admittedly, but since the end of hostilities there has been such a bustle on Level 7 that life here seems different.

P thinks it is the therapy which has made the improvement in me. She may be right, but I am sure the radio communication with other levels has something to do with it too. That is how it seems to me, anyway.

I think that if we had had the radio links all the time, from the very beginning, I would never have collapsed. I said so to X-107, but he had his usual sound argument against such an arrangement. "If we'd been able to talk to the outside world all the time," he said, "we'd have longed to get out. That would have slowed down our adjustment to Level 7. But now that nobody in his right mind would dream of changing his privileged position down here, contact with other levels can only do us good."

132

He was right, of course.

Today we heard some very interesting political news. The enemy denied our claim to victory and said that he had won the war. His arguments, and our politicians' counter-arguments, were quite ingenious.

The enemy maintained that he had succeeded in destroying our country before we destroyed his. His last missiles were fired before 11.00 hours, whereas we pushed our last buttons at 11.20.

Our people admitted this, but interpreted it the opposite way. They said that he who fired the last shot was the victor. The enemy, they suggested, could not fire the last of his missiles at all, because his launching sites had been put out of order by our rockets.

That was not so, said the enemy, promptly resorting to another sort of argument: as he was fighting for the right and ultimately victorious cause, he said, he must have been victorious.

We maintained precisely the same for our cause and ourselves.

Then the politicians started slinging mud at each other. I do not remember all the abusive phrases they used, but here are some of them.

They called each other 'war criminals', 'inhuman beasts', 'beastly men', 'unprogressive', 'reactionary', 'selfish', 'child murderers' and 'arch-criminals of human history'. They also exchanged such honours as 'barbarian mongols' and 'beastly successors of red-skins', as well as 'hangmen of humanity' and 'electrocutioners of mankind'.

To cut a long story (it *is* long, it is still going on) short: the war continues! The military levels on both sides are doing nothing. But from their respective caves the politicians fire insults at each other through the intercontinental radio transmitters.

For all practical purposes, the war is over. The destruction appears to be immense. The enemy and we, his satellites and our allies (or, as he prefers to put his, his allies and our satellites), indeed the entire surface of the earth, have been laid in ruins.

Even the neutral countries seem to have suffered heavy losses. Somehow they got hit too, by both our rockets and the enemy's. Out of the thousands that were fired, quite a few missed their targets. So the neutrals suffered because of the lack of perfection in the guiding mechanism of the intercontinental rocket. It is a pity, in a way, but obviously it could not be helped.

Some heavily populated and underdeveloped neutral countries could not afford to build any shelters, and so perished completely. Others, better off, were well prepared for the danger and probably had better shelters for the mass of their population than we had.

Anyway, we can now listen to their broadcasts. They accuse both sides of lack of humanity. Sometimes what they say resembles the criticism which comes down from the cranks on Level 2.

But who can be blamed for the damage that has been caused? If global war is waged with intercontinental missiles equipped with thermonuclear warheads, the relatively small neutral countries cannot help getting hurt.

Besides, why should they be spared suffering, if the major powers are destroyed? Are they any better? They are certainly a lot weaker!

The neutrals go on reproaching the two great powers. They claim that the big two are morally responsible for the annihilation of their respective allies. And they say the big two had no right to drag neutral countries into the abyss of destruction.

Our broadcasting service on Level 5 answers some of the charges. It says that we acted purely in self-defence, and that all the blame should be laid at the enemy's door. *"Everybody has the right to survive,"* said the head of our government earlier today, "and that is precisely the reason why we had to defend ourselves against the treacherous assault of the enemy. For the right to survival implies the right to self-defence!"

The neutral broadcaster took up this argument, drawing opposite conclusions: "In the atomic age," he said, "survival cannot be safeguarded by self-defence: for self-defence with thermonuclear weapons means *total* destruction."

There are other neutral countries which do not join in these discussions, but broadcast accounts of the destruction. Some stress the human angle, going on incessantly about the great suffering caused, the number of people assumed dead all over the world. "Humanity has been decimated," one speaker said. "Indeed, 'decimated' is not the word for it: out of a world population of about three thousand million people, the estimated number of survivors is only a few millions. Perhaps twenty million, perhaps fifteen or ten. And even these are condemned to live in caves!"

These were pretty gloomy statements, but somehow I did not feel as sorry for humanity as the speaker seemed to. 'All right,' I thought, 'so there will be less human beings on earth. What difference does that make? Why is it better to have more people rather than less? And as for living in caves, well,

I've grown to accept the life I'm forced to live down here, so why should other people expect to be able to walk in the sunshine? That wouldn't be fair, would it?'

Other neutrals bewail, not the decease of a large number of human beings, but what they call "the catastrophic decline of civilisation": "Libraries and museums, works of art, institutes of learning, houses, monuments, railways, roads, factories—all these are a thing of the past. What remains now and for the future is shelters, caves, bare minimal existence for the few survivors." Another one added: "The toil of centuries, the traditions of generations, the wisdom of ages—all blown away in a few split seconds of atomic blast. This is the suicide of civilisation!"

This kind of talk is rather alien to my way of thinking. Perhaps I have become biased by living so long underground. Or perhaps the psychological treatment did something to make me immune to such appeals. For one reason or another, all these descriptions and arguments mean nothing to me.

Libraries have been destroyed. So what? Museums are in ashes. Who wants to visit a museum anyway? The traditions of centuries perished in a moment. Who cares about traditions?

Maybe I was not so unfeeling when I still lived on the surface, though I was picked for my job because I was pretty unsociable. Up there I might have felt differently. But down here—who cares?

It could be that this is one of the reasons why PBX Command was placed underground. I think that even if it had been possible to construct a safe shelter outside—a round dome of thick glass, say, which would allow us to see the world—it would have been a very unwise thing to do. For psychological reasons, as well as for physical security, we had to be sent below if our performance was to be reliable.

Who knows?—if I had been able to see the world and the destruction I was causing, I might have recoiled from pushing the buttons, just as X-117 did when it came to A4, B4 and C4.

No news of him, incidentally.

JUNE 17

The neutral countries have been asking us and the enemy to tell them what metals were used for the casings of the rigged bombs. They want to know so that they can estimate the time they will have to spend in their shelters. Radioactivity can last anything from a few seconds to millenniums, depending on the material; so the knowledge of what metals were used may certainly be of practical significance. What they are anxious to find out is whether they will be able to go up fairly soon, or have to stay underground indefinitely.

Both we and the enemy have refused to tell them what we used. The reason given was that this was a military secret which might benefit the other side.

The neutrals tried to bargain with both sides, stressing the shortage of their underground supplies. We both declared ourselves ready to make the secret known, provided the other side did so too.

But I do not see how this can work out in practice. There is the problem of who will disclose the information first. And even if both sides agree to disclose it simultaneously, as a statesman from one neutral country has suggested, it is still doubtful whether the enemy will tell the truth.

The enemy suspects our honesty too. He says we may give false information in order to make people leave their caves and be killed by radioactivity.

So on this issue there is complete deadlock.

There is news about X-117. They have had trouble with him. After that collapse on duty, he somehow relapsed into his neurotic state and the psychologists have given up trying to cure him. Perhaps because his services are no longer needed.

He has developed a guilt complex. He thinks he is responsible for the destruction of the world. As if he could not have been replaced by anybody else! He actually *was* replaced. But there is no arguing with a neurotic.

Today P and I visited him in his room—out of politeness. He lives opposite me and we worked together, after all. And P treated him when he was ill the first time.

X-117 was lying on his bed, half dressed, unshaven, doing nothing. When we came in, he hardly seemed to notice it.

P asked him how he felt. For some reason this enraged him. He suddenly sat up on the bed and shouted at us: "Thank you! I feel fine! I feel wonderful! I've succeeded in killing hundreds of millions of people, so I feel on top of the world. I'm the greatest hangman in history! Why shouldn't I feel well?"

Then he burst into tears. I had never seen anything like it before. He cried like a little boy whose plaything had been snatched away. He just sat there racked by loud sobs.

P tried to calm him. "You shouldn't feel that way," she said. "You just did your duty. Are you a soldier or aren't you?"

X-117 answered, tears rolling down his face: "Duty? Can there be a duty to kill humanity? To be mankind's hangman?"

"But you're not responsible for the killing," I told him. "Why call yourself a hangman? You just obeyed orders."

"So does the hangman," was his answer. "But at least he obeys an order given by a judge. I did what a robot told me to do!" At this he started laughing, as hysterically as he had wept before.

"But look," said P, "my husband did just what you did—in fact he went on obeying orders after you had left. And he doesn't feel the least bit guilty."

"As a matter of fact," I added, "I feel better now than I did before. Not that I enjoyed pushing those buttons particularly, but doing it made me feel rather important."

"Oh, you poor fool!" he retorted. "How dare you even think about yourself after the crime you've committed? *Your* feelings! As if they matter. You've murdered millions of people—blasted, burned, poisoned *hundreds* of millions! Do you know what that means? And now you talk about how *you* feel! You monster!"

I thought he was going to hit me, but he did not. Somehow I did not mind his antagonistic attitude. I dare say that if one is not sociable, one neither loves nor hates. And perhaps the psychological treatment has left me with even fewer emotions than I had before.

But what he said reminded me of the chilly feeling I had had when I saw the black screen in the Operations Room. The feeling had passed and had not recurred, even when I heard the details of the destruction, but I remembered it clearly. And I had not been back to that room since. So perhaps X-117's reaction made some sense, even though I could not share it.

I was preoccupied with these thoughts when X-117 started shouting and wailing again: "Why? Why did I do it? Why did I push those buttons and kill them all? So many! . . ."

P motioned to me that we should go now. X-117 saw her sign and turned on her, shouting: "So you've had enough of this visit, you psychologist, you soul-killer! You managed to cure me of my conscience so that I'd be able to kill humanity. And you did the same to your husband. He might have had some conscience before! Now I've done my duty, you don't need me any more. Soul-killer!" He stood up and waved his arms at us. "Get out of this room! Both of you! Go on, get out—before I strangle you! Not kill you with a button, no! With my bare hands! . . ."

We left before he finished his ravings.

JUNE 19

X-117 was found dead this morning.

His room-mate had woken to find X-117 missing from his bed. But his uniform was still there, so X-137m had got up and opened the door to see where he had gone. He found him just down the corridor, hanging by a belt from a pipe which runs across the top of the Operations Room doorway. X-107 and I were woken up by X-137m's tapping on our door.

I saw his body dangling there, the unshaven face and the glazed half-mad eyes.

I saw him for a split second only, for I turned my head away quickly and walked back into my room, closing the door behind me. Again I had that chilly feeling, and I shivered as I had done when I saw the black screen.

The other two must have pushed the red button, for a minute later I heard footsteps outside the door and the murmur of voices. Then X-107 came back and quietly lay down on his bed. Another two minutes passed, and then the private loudspeaker sounded. We were instructed not to tell anybody what we had seen.

An hour later the general loudspeaker system announced that Push-Button Officer X-117 had died in the night. The speaker said something about 'loyal service' and the 'strain' which had been placed on his constitution by the 'vital task' he had performed during the recent offensive.

I suppose they are quite right to conceal the fact that this was suicide. Why depress people?

But why did he hang himself? I have been asking myself

140

the question all day long. What was the trouble with him? He was rather a pleasant fellow before he became mentally unbalanced. I feel rather sorry for him.

When I saw P today it was all I could do to prevent myself telling her the true facts, particularly when she expressed her puzzlement at what the loudspeaker had said. While she had had X-117 under observation, she said, he had never given any sign of physical weakness.

I kept a check on my tongue, however, and we just discussed X-117 in a general way. She said I should not allow my fellow button-pusher's death to depress me. It was the best thing that could have happened to him, she said, because he was quite the wrong person for life on Level 7. He must have been chosen by mistake.

While she was talking I heard again the words X-117 used yesterday, his last day alive. He had not accepted the inevitable. He had rebelled against it. He had not become adjusted to reality as it was. He was different. He was certainly not the right man for Level 7.

It is odd that I should feel sorrier for X-117 than for those thousands of millions killed in the war. I believe that if I had been told to push a button which would execute X-117, I could not have done it. Though without thinking twice about it I pushed the buttons which executed millions!

Executed? Am I a hangman? X-117 said we were hangmen. In a way, we were. Perhaps he was right and not P.

No, I still do not believe I could be a hangman. I do not enjoy contact with people who are going to die soon. I have no liking for the sight of life disappearing, bodies hanging. Like his.

But to push a button, to operate a 'typewriter'—that is a very different thing. It is smooth, clean, mechanical.

That is where X-117 went wrong. For him it was the same thing. He could even talk about strangling P and me with his bare hands!

141

Maybe this inability to distinguish between killing with the bare hands and pushing a button was the source of his mental trouble.

JUNE 20

There is some alarming news from Level 2. A few days ago they broadcast that everyone was suffering from some sort of disease. The symptoms were nausea and vomiting, and severe diarrhoea. The fact that *everybody* had caught it at the same time seemed suspicious, but the symptoms must have disappeared because the matter was not mentioned again, the broadcasts reverting to their customary abuse of the government.

Today, though, they say the symptoms have come back and are even more distressing. People are emaciated and feverish. And similar reports are coming over the radio from the neutral countries. There too, the sickness appears to be general. In the middle of one broadcast the speaker himself broke off in mid-sentence, and we could hear him vomiting quite clearly. It was awful. Somebody else had to take over.

Radio reports from Level 2 started to come in again while I was writing that. I will try to jot down what the man says.

People are dying. "Like flies" (his very words!). He is shouting: "It's your bloody radioactivity! You've poisoned us too!"

They are going over to a big hall, or something, in one of the shelters. Now I can distinctly hear groaning and vomiting. Nobody is saying anything—too weak, perhaps.

Broadcaster again: "Hundreds of people . . . lying on floor . . . no help at all . . . nobody capable of helping . . . some are vomiting . . . diarrhoea . . . horrible stench."

He has stopped to cough and blow his nose.

He goes on: "Some seem to be dead already . . . many un-

conscious . . . perhaps dead too, nobody to check . . . makes
no difference . . . everyone will die sooner or later . . . matter of hours . . . some perhaps a day or two . . . no difference. . . ."

I missed something there, his voice suddenly grew very
weak. He has turned away from the microphone to be sick
or something. I can hear groans again, louder.

He says: "I can't go on."

That's all.

No, he is trying to say something else. He has to speak very
slowly.

"Our shelter is becoming a grave, a collective grave of human misery." Louder now: "Politicians! Soldiers! From the
bottom of our grave we curse you! May you follow in our
. . ." His voice fails him.

"Steps," I suppose he wanted to say. But there is nothing
coming over except groans and the sound of people vomiting.

Now the station has been switched off.

JUNE 21

The news is the same as yesterday's: neutrals and Level 2
are dying fast.

The probable reason for these deaths is polluted air. The
filters used on Level 2 and in the neutral countries are apparently not a good enough protection against radioactivity
—at least, against the strong dose they have just received. Nobody knows for certain, and nobody is going up to make sure.
But there seems no doubt that millions of people have escaped death by blast or burning only to die of poisoned air.

This means that the world population is quickly being reduced to those living in the deeper levels, the ones fitted with
self-sufficient air-supply systems. The enemy must have shelters with this equipment too, but I suppose none of the allies
and neutrals could afford it. If nothing happens to halt the

143

present death-rate, the population will drop in a matter of days—perhaps hours—to a mere one and a third millions. Maybe a few thousands more or less for the enemy's deep shelters may differ in capacity from ours.

Nothing has been heard from the neutrals since about 14.00 hours, when the last of their messages was received. It gave facts and figures, in some detail, about the mass deaths. It did not end in the pathetic way yesterday's Level 2 broadcast did. But the dry report, trying to give the up-to-date figures of death—as if life would go on there tomorrow—was, in a way, even more pathetic. There were no accusations, no curses in this broadcast: just the latest news about the victims of radioactivity in that country.

It went off the air quite suddenly. There have been no more neutral broadcasts since. There will be no more.

Of all the people who used to live on this earth, only we and our enemy remain. To be more precise: only that handful on each side which is deep underground.

JUNE 22

There is a strange feeling in the air—other people besides myself have noticed it, and perhaps it is not restricted to Level 7—a feeling that we are living in a new world.

The old world, on the surface of the globe and on the underground levels connected with or dependent on the surface —that world is dead. Life has been restricted to those who went deep enough and who are self-sufficient, even in the matter of their air-supply.

The surface of the earth is out of bounds, definitely and absolutely so. And will be for some time to come. How long, is a matter for debate. More and more people can be heard discussing the question. The neutrals asked it, and got no answer. Not that it would have made any difference to their fate, for death was already in their bodies.

But we, who have all the equipment to keep ourselves alive down here, we want to know the answer.

Strontium 90's half-life, the time taken for its radioactivity to decay to half its original strength, is twenty-five years. The half-life of Uranium 239 is twenty-three minutes. But Uranium 238's half-life is 4,510,000,000 years! Which of the isotopes is poisoning the surface?

The answer to that question will decide the life of the remaining levels. We on Level 7 are best off, with supplies for 500 years. Go up to Level 5, and the underground life-span drops to 200 years. While in only twenty-five years the inhabitants of Level 3 will be forced to leave their burrows and risk life on the surface!

It is certain that surface pollution was intended to last for years. Otherwise the Button 4 bombs would not have been used at all. But years, decades or centuries?

People on Level 3 have raised the question in very practical terms. Though a life expectancy of twenty-five years is pretty good, if you remember that most of humanity has just died, they still face a problem. They are asking: "Should we raise children?" Children born now on Level 3 will starve in the prime of their life, unless they can get out.

So for them it is a significant problem. And so it is, in a less pressing way, for all the rest of us cave-dwellers. Even we, on Level 7, would like to know the answer. Can we look forward to the prospect of going out before we die? And if not, will our descendants be able to go out in five centuries' time? The fate of remote descendants cannot be said to affect us personally; but we are curious to know whether humanity has a chance to survive and, perhaps, one day spread again over the face of the globe.

In the lounge today, in the dining-hall, in corridors and rooms where people met and passed the time of day, the same question was on everyone's lips or, unspoken, in their eyes: how long will the surface be radioactive?

On other levels they go so far as to ask the question over the air, time and again. Perhaps because they are not so well adjusted to living underground.

Anyway, no one on Level 7 can give them the answer they keep asking for. Somebody on Level 5 must be able to, and Level 5 has been specifically requested to supply the information. But they give evasive replies, not a clear answer.

They advise Level 3 *against* begetting children, certainly; which must mean that in twenty-five years the deluge will not be over. They also say that living underground is safe and that we should not think about the surface; which implies something about how long the radioactivity will last.

They say it all depends on what kind of material the enemy used for his rigged bombs. What they do not tell us is what stuff *we* used. All this sounds very mysterious. Why the hell can't they tell the truth, or at least that part of the truth which they know?

If we could contact them, those leaders of ours, we would get the truth pretty soon. There are ways of squeezing it out of men without using atomic bombs. But we are here, and they are there, and the only contact is by radio. So there is nothing we can do.

It is obvious that they do not want to give us this information. It is equally clear that for immediate practical purposes the information is of no significance: we are down here for life.

My guess is that the truth is worse than many people think. Otherwise our leaders would tell us all they knew. But they do not, perhaps because they are ashamed. Or maybe they are repentant.

To hell with them, anyway! We cannot get a thing out of them.

JUNE 24

Level 3 reports that a married couple there have decided to go out tomorrow and take a look at the world. They do not want to stay inside for the rest of their lives. In fact they do not want to remain underground a day longer.

I remember I felt that way sometimes before I had my psychological treatment.

They intend to take a radio transmitter with them and report on what they see. Everybody down here looks forward with keen interest to that, and I suppose people must be just as curious on Level 3, or they would not allow this suicidal enterprise.

Because it *is* suicide. That pair will never come back. They must perish on this trip, and they know it perfectly well. But they will have a few days out in the sun.

Everyone on Level 7 is talking about this business. Some people think they are mad. Others say they are brave. If I am not mistaken, everyone envies them a little. Perhaps because of the publicity. Or because of the sunshine.

It is P's firm opinion that they are neurotic—though even she seems to look forward with some eagerness to this strange escapade.

JUNE 25

They are out.

Their first report was that they had found several cars in good condition inside the underground mouth to their shelter.

147

They chose the best and filled the back seat with cans of petrol which owners of some of the other cars had brought with them —no doubt in the vain hope that they would be able to drive back to their (non-existent) homes even if all the filling stations went up in smoke. This gives them enough fuel for a week's drive at least. Food and water they took with them from the shelter.

The man is driving while his wife works the transmitter. Judging by what she says, the shelter was not very close to a burst. Even so, everything around has been scorched by fire. The road is in relatively good condition.

She says she will broadcast again in half an hour.

They are driving in the direction of a small town. As they go on, the way is becoming more difficult. Débris is scattered over the road. But the car they picked has good tyres, the woman says, so they are going on.

Reckoning by the mileage covered, she says, they should have reached the town by now. But there is nothing to indicate that they have. There used to be a church there which dominated the view. They should have seen the tower long ago. But there is nothing, absolutely nothing. Even the quantity of débris is quite small. Everything must have burned.

There are signs of fire to confirm this, she says. The destruction is so complete that it is hard to believe that anything ever stood where they are now.

Nor do they see anything on the horizon. They are driving through fairly flat country, with no hills to obscure the view, but there is nothing to be seen. Other roads keep crossing theirs, but that is all. Here and there the road is severely damaged, but if they drive carefully they can get over the bad patches. They have to go slowly.

Now the woman says they are faced with a serious obstacle: part of the road ahead has cracked up to become quite impassable. She will break off her broadcast while she helps her husband to find a detour.

Quarter of an hour later: she says they managed to go round and get back on their road. They are keen to reach ground zero, the actual point where a bomb burst, but if the roads are that poor it will be impossible to do it by car. They could have done it if they had had a helicopter. The woman says they will be forced to take the best roads available and just see where they lead to.

She will broadcast more news this afternoon at 14.00 hours.

. . . . .

The afternoon broadcast has just finished. It started late, at about 14.15 hours. The reason, the woman explained, was that they had both been ill.

She had been the first to feel unwell, and when her nausea turned to vomiting they had to stop. This happened only a few minutes after her previous broadcast, when they had not been out of the shelter more than an hour and a half.

After she had rested they drove on, but they had not gone far before her husband had an attack of the same sort. Nausea. Stop the car. Vomiting. Diarrhoea. The old story.

The woman said they know it means radiation sickness, but they do not mind. They intend to go on and cover as much distance as they can before nightfall, as soon as her husband has rested. They will not use the transmitter again until they have some interesting news, she says.

JUNE 26

This escapade has caused incredible excitement—on all levels, apparently. Everybody is following the radio reports from outside. People are going without sleep so as not to miss broadcasts. And even when the two outside are not reporting —resting or asleep—discussion still goes on down here.

There has never, since the day we came down, been such excitement on Level 7. Not even during the war—or so people say. (I was not able to judge what effect the war had: I was busy conducting it.)

People are intrigued to know even the smallest personal details about the pair. Who are they? How old are they? What were their occupations? Where are they from? Do they have relatives down below? And so on.

He is an artist, a landscape painter. His wife has no particular job.

"This helps to explain why they decided to go up," some people say. "There's not much landscape underground."

"There's not much left outside either," others retort. Still, the man must have felt dreadful in a crowded, enclosed shelter.

There is another fact which may have something to do with their escapade. They had expected to meet their eighteen-year-old daughter in the shelter. She had been assigned to the same one as they. When the warning siren sounded she was away from home, visiting a friend. They phoned her and she assured them she would come straight to the shelter. But they never found her there. There must have been an accident. Nobody will ever know what happened. Obviously mishaps like that are bound to occur in such large operations: millions of people rushing, panic-stricken, to their respective shelters—or to *any* shelter.

So now the parents are outside, not looking for their daughter, but preferring to shorten their lives and die where they were born, in the sunshine.

I have just listened to their latest report. She is driving now, while he does the talking.

They feel more or less all right again. This often happens with radiation sickness. After the initial shock, nausea, vomiting and diarrhoea, a few symptom-free days may follow. But the symptoms will come back.

They are driving on all the time. But there is not much to report. Every now and then they see the remains of a steel

frame sticking out of the ground, sometimes twisted into a
strange shape. One such piece seemed to catch the painter's
imagination. He found it beautiful and said it would be quite
in place in a museum of modern art. He thought an appropriate title would be 'The Martyred Steel'.

They are good reporters, both of them. They do not drama-
tise. Certainly they are not melodramatic. They do not shed
tears, they just report facts. With a little artistic colouring
added.

Only there is so little to report. Complete destruction is
complete destruction. To try to describe how complete such
complete destruction is, is to be reduced to playing with
words—or with what was and is no more.

But these two are not playing. They are looking for something that may have been spared. And all they can find is a
tortured steel frame.

JUNE 27

They are still driving on and reporting, though they complain of fatigue.

This morning they came across a Level 1 shelter, a rather
shallow and relatively small one. It must have been a good
way from a ground zero, but there were cracks in the concrete
roof. They tried to get into the shelter, but the entrance was
blocked by big chunks of concrete and steel, so they had to
give up. There was nobody still alive there, of course. Still, it
would have been interesting to know whether the people inside had died of blast, burns or radiation.

As the couple go on, their reports are becoming less fre-
quent. Because they feel tired, and because there is nothing
to report.

People down here are rather disappointed. This trip to the

surface seems to be a very boring affair, even more boring than life underground!

The people who thought the whole idea rather silly at the outset have started calling them cranks again. "Fools, to be more precise," said P when we met this afternoon. "Fancy paying for such a boring trip with twenty-five years of life! Behaviour like that isn't just neurotic, it's plain folly."

Interest in the escapade wanes steadily. It is still the main topic of conversation, but it is no longer discussed with quite the same fervour as before.

If their trip goes on for a few more days, people will probably give up listening to their scanty reports altogether. They will die for us even before they are really dead.

JUNE 28

The brave and foolish pair have decided to stop where they are and go no farther. They themselves seem to be bored. The scene in one place is identical with the scene any where else. There is no point in moving around. Even if they could circle the world, it would probably be the same story. They must have realised that.

And they are exhausted—tired by the driving and weakened by the sickness within them.

So they just sit in the car, resting, and occasionally transmitting some personal impressions. These become less and less descriptive and more and more emotional as time goes on. At times almost poetic—or perhaps delirious. They must be an interesting pair. And very sick by now.

There is something about the quality of these occasional talks which makes people listen again. Interest in the couple revives—interest in them personally, rather than in the surface of the earth.

Here comes one of their talks now. I will try to scribble

152

down their exact words. It all sounds pretty odd. Delirious already, perhaps.

She: "We're a pair of doves, sent out by Noah to see if the flood has gone down."

He: "The flood is still around us, the water is deep. We're the doves which *didn't* fly back."

She: "But the dove which didn't return to Noah was a sign that the flood was over. It was a sign of life and hope when it stayed away from the ark."

He: "How right you are, my dove! We'll stay here, outside the shelter, until it's all over. For this is a much worse flood than the one God made. Men caused this tide of blood to rise and leave no hope for man or dove."

She: "Listen to us, you people down there in the caves. Hear what we have to tell you. The flood is around you, the poison is trying to get inside you. Your blood is still red, but the world is black. Stay below in your man-made caves as long as there is air to breathe, as long as water seeps so deep, as long as spirits don't go down and drag you up!"

He: "Stay in the ark for ever!"

They must certainly be delirious. But not everyone in delirium can talk that way. It is broadcasts like that one which have people listening, fascinated. Almost everybody. Even P has stopped making disparaging remarks. After one of this morning's transmissions I do believe I saw an unusual shine in her eyes. As if they were wet.

JUNE 29

The couple are still broadcasting, though their voices are weaker today and they have to break off from time to time. But we listen. Everybody listens.

Another broadcast is due to start any moment now. I will

153

try to jot down what they say as I did yesterday. It is easier now that they have to speak slower.

She: "No birds are singing in the world today, no flowers are blooming. There are no trees, there are no fields."
He: "Just débris."
She: "Man is gone, and woman too. No children play around."
He: "Just bare earth."
She: "The world is like a ship abandoned by her crew. Like the moon, it is arid and dreary."
He: "Another planet."

Another planet. They have got something there. In their delirium they may have hit on a truth. The earth *has* become like the dead moon—except for the caves. But who knows?— there may be caves like ours on the moon, with some crawling creatures living in them.

Just another planet. The earth was always that, anyway. But not just that: for there were other things on earth.

JUNE 30

The couple announced today that they would not broadcast any more. They are too weak. They ended like this:

He: "This is our last message, the last broadcast from the face of the earth. Nothing new to report. The world is empty. It still revolves. There is day and night, sun and moon and stars. But that is all."
She: "Farewell, men and women of the caves! Let us die in peace."

That was this morning. Since then nothing has been heard

154

from them. I wonder if they are delirious or unconscious. Perhaps they are gone already.

We shall not hear from them again. Let them die in peace.

I did not intend adding to what I had written earlier today. But although the time is already past 23.00 (I have reverted to normal hours for sleeping since my daily duty finished), I do not want to go to bed until I have recorded a strange feeling which has come over me since hearing that last broadcast. The feeling is new to me, yet not entirely strange: a feeling of tenderness for those two up there in the car. I wish I could have comforted them and helped them.

Something seems to have changed inside me. It stirred when I saw X-117 hanging, just outside in the corridor there; but on that occasion the sensation quickly passed. Perhaps my new feeling is connected with the sudden chill I felt then, and earlier, when I saw the black screen. But this is different: not a passing shiver, but a persistent warmth.

Is this compassion? Love? Sociability? Are other human beings able to arouse in me feelings like those? Was there a green spot hidden in my soul which they, the doves, have discovered?

It is a warm feeling—warm towards them. But it has enough warmth for humanity in general, for any living thing. It even reflects back to keep me warm inside.

Only now do I realise how *cold* I was inside. How dead. Now I can understand X-117. He must have had a lot of that warm feeling. It could not have been taken from him, even by psychotherapy.

I do not have *that* much. But I have some, enough to keep me warm. And chilly too, in a curious way, when I think of that screen, or even of the buttons which blackened it.

One needs that warmth in order to feel chilly. And it is better to feel warm and cold than not to feel at all. That is what the treatment they gave me was supposed to do: deprive me of what little feeling I might have possessed.

155

But they failed. I love that pair of doves, dying out there on the bare planet. I love them.

If there can be such a pair of doves, the planet will live again. If I can love, then my soul is not like the dead shell of a planet. It can be revived.

Life and love are spreading. Give them a little space to take root, a beginning, and they will conquer the world!

JULY 1

What nonsense I wrote last night. "Life and love are spreading!"

Death and destruction, hate and indifference—these are spreading. It is not a pair of doves which has conquered the world: buttons have done that. They have killed everything. Even the doves.

That feeling inside me—what can it do? Unpush the pushed buttons? Unrelease the released rockets? Unbomb the bombed world? Undestroy the destroyed? Unkill the killed? Save a pair of doves?

It can do nothing. The buttons have been pushed. It is too late! Too late!

JULY 2

No more broadcasts from the couple up there. They are probably dead by now. People have stopped talking about them. They pass into oblivion.

But *I* still think about them. They are alive for me. They have pushed the hidden button in my soul. The lost, forgotten, decayed button. It was a hard thing to do, but they did it.

What a wonderful button it is. It makes me realise that I am not alone in the world. It makes me feel that there are other beings like myself. Better than myself, some of them:

X-117 was better. And the people who stayed outside—most of them were probably better than I.

Why is it so difficult to push that button of humanity, and so easy to push the ones which launch deadly rockets? And why did nobody discover my good button earlier, before it was all too late?

Not that it would have affected the results. If I had refused to push the buttons, and X-117 had refused, X-107 and X-137m would have done it. And if they had refused, anybody else could have done it—without even knowing what he was doing!

The same results could have been achieved without using the Operations Room at all. Our rockets could have been released automatically the moment the enemy rockets exploded, and vice versa. The retaliatory arrangement was *almost* automatic as it was. It could easily have been made *completely* automatic. It was an automatic error which started the war. From that point the chain reaction could have gone on with automatic perfection to destroy the world, without any of us button-pushers raising a finger to help it.

When all that has been said, at the bottom of this super-clever, super-stupid business there still remain some human beings in whose souls a button remains unpushed. As mine was, till now.

But what could be done about it? How could all those other buttons be pushed to release the humanity which everyone perhaps has somewhere inside him?

Still, why bother about it? It is too late anyhow.

❖   ❖   ❖   ❖   ❖

SEPTEMBER 13

Yesterday part of my diary was destroyed. P, in a fit of temper, grabbed a sizeable chunk and tore it to bits. I did

157

not bother to stop her. Why should I? The world went to pieces: should I care what happens to my diary?

P cannot understand me—or rather, the change in me since that couple from Level 3 went up. She says she could put up with me when I was gloomy, depressed, mentally ill. "But," to quote her, "in this saintly shape of yours I just can't stand you."

What seems to enrage her most is the fact that I do not retaliate by storming back at her. My meekness makes her more furious than ever, though it is not intended to. I just do not find in myself any anger against her—or against anybody else, for that matter.

This is neither saintly nor vicious. Something in me has changed, that is all. I do not undergo the mental ups and downs which troubled me before; my mood is on one level. I have no need of company and entertainment. Nor even the speculation I used to indulge in. My thoughts often ramble through the world that is gone, though, and I think a good deal about humanity—the humanity that disappeared during those few hours of button-pushing.

I think about all these things calmly, in a detached way, yet sympathetically. I feel no pangs of conscience or remorse, though. I do not know why.

P does not understand this mood of mine. I suppose she cannot classify it according to the psychology she has learnt. She was waiting patiently in the hope that it would change, I think, until yesterday's incident, which made her lose her temper. It happened during her visit to my room. (Such visits have been allowed since hostilities ended.) She must have thought that tearing my diary would be some kind of shock to me, for when I failed to react she shouted: "Oh, if that didn't shake you, nothing will!" Then she spun on her heel and left the room without giving me another glance.

The last entry in the diary to survive P's assault was the one for July 2. More than two months have elapsed since then.

158

I am not going to rewrite what I wrote during that time. Not much happened, anyway; and my inner changes—well, I doubt if they would interest my prospective readers (if I have any).

Perhaps one thing should be mentioned, though it was already clear back in June. The living world has shrunk, shrunk incredibly, into a few holes. But these holes—Levels 3, 4, 5, 6 and 7, with an estimated 622,500 people—go on living. I do not know what precisely is the situation in the enemy's country, the number of levels and people surviving there; but probably the population of the whole world is now somewhere between one and two millions. Incredibly small, but also extremely dense, if one remembers the limited space available underground.

Still, it is amazing how people can adjust themselves to the new conditions. Now, three months after A-Day ('A' for Atomic War), life seems to be smoothly regulated even on the civilian levels.

How flexible human beings are! And yet how rigid!

SEPTEMBER 14

P announced this morning that she wanted to divorce me and marry X-107. He had often been present when she visited me in my room, and that is how they had got to know each other.

I agreed and wished her better luck with her new mate. She had tears in her eyes.

X-107 was rather uneasy about it, but I told him I did not mind at all, and this seemed to reassure him.

The formalities were arranged for this afternoon without any difficulty. P and I were divorced in the marriage-cum-laundry room, where five minutes later she was married to X-107. I was told to leave the 'm' from my identity badge in the room. X-107 probably got it.

I think this development was inevitable and for the best. Perhaps a man of so-called 'saintly' disposition should not be married.

    .   .   .   .   .

The general loudspeaker announced today that the PBX Operations Room was to be transformed into a maternity ward. Several births are expected, but not before January or February next year, so there is plenty of time and no real need to announce the conversion of the room so early.

Perhaps the news was given now with the intention of cheering people up. They even tried to suggest that the transformation is symbolical: from operations room, the centre of push-button war, into maternity ward, the place where new life starts.

"And you shall beat your push-buttons into perambulators," occurred to me.

Rather late in the day, though!

I rarely go to the lounge now. There is nobody I want to talk to. People I meet there, my fellow-internees on Level 7, think differently, feel differently. I might have found a good companion in X-117. But he is gone. Not by blast or fire or radioactivity. By his own hand and a leather belt.

But I commune with myself. I almost converse with the artist and his wife who chose to die their radioactive death.

There are people living all round me, but I do not live with them. For me the dead are alive. The living are dead.

SEPTEMBER 15

Alarming news from Level 3. There are symptoms of radioactive sickness there.

The first signs appeared yesterday, the broadcast said; but they decided to say nothing about it until they were sure what was wrong. By now the symptoms are so widespread that no doubt remains. Somehow radioactivity has reached Level 3.

There are several theories as to how it happened. The most plausible one is that the water supply has been polluted. Water for Level 3 and below comes from ground sources and is naturally filtered by the earth layers through which it passes. But perhaps the filtering is not thorough enough. Who knows? The system was never tested under the extreme conditions which have existed since A-Day.

There were so many underground explosions. In numerous places the earth must have been polluted down to a considerable depth. In such spots, perhaps, the rain water has been contaminated rather than filtered on its way to the ground water sources.

Well, I really do not know how this calamity has come about, but it has happened all right. Eighteen shelters on Level 3 are affected by radioactivity. They are probably doomed.

Some people I spoke to today were seriously worried. For Level 3 is self-sufficient, a part of the new underground world. If *they* are being poisoned, say the pessimists, *anyone* can be poisoned.

The optimists retort that the differences in depth are significant and decisive. Otherwise Levels 4, 5, 6 and 7 would never have been built. The deeper the level, the safer. Level 7's water supply passes through many more natural filters than Level 3's.

SEPTEMBER 16

The optimists have been over-confident. Reports of sickness have come in from six shelters on Level 4 and two on Level 5. Four more shelters on Level 3 are affected.

All three levels have been ordered to distil all their drinking water. It is not enough to boil it: they must distil it. I do not know how they will set about doing that, for they have no special equipment for the job. But they will have to manage somehow—or else go on drinking poisoned water.

The military levels, 6 and 7, are all right. Our water supply comes from a really great depth.

SEPTEMBER 17

The news from Levels 3, 4 and 5 is terrible. Everybody is coming down with severe symptoms. Yesterday some of the shelters on these levels were still all right. Today there is not one unpoisoned shelter, and reports of deaths have already started to come in.

They are distilling their water, but it looks as if the damage has already been done. The precautions may have been taken in time to save some, perhaps. We shall know in a week or two. Perhaps sooner. It does not take long to find out.

Not so long ago this news would not have affected me at all. Now I feel sorry for those people up there. It must be horrible for them, knowing their probable fate and not being able to do a thing about it. Those who are still able to get about can busy themselves with hopefully distilling the water. Apart from that, all they can do is wait and see.

If Levels 3, 4 and 5 perish, only the military levels will be left. The ex-PBX and ex-PBY Commands. But now our job will be not to destroy but to create: to ensure the survival of mankind.

Can people who helped to destroy become creative? What kind of humanity can the men and women who were once PBX Command give birth to? PBY Command was purely defensive. But we are the hangmen of mankind, as X-117 so aptly called us. And are we to form the *élite* which will perpetuate the human race?

What will it be like, this race? Our children will never see sunshine. They will never get inspiration from beautiful

162

things, as those two doves did. If human beings who had known life under the sky could degenerate into creatures crawling about underground, what hope have people who never saw day and night, who never smelled a flower?

X-107 suggested, when I told him what I had been thinking, that our children and our children's children may be taken to see plants growing in the air-supply department.

"Well, that may be so, but. . . ."

SEPTEMBER 18

In one of the shelters on Level 5 there is rioting. Our leaders, statesmen and politicians, are there sharing the lot of the others. But some people want to take personal vengeance on them. They say the leaders are to blame for the disaster.

They have done it. One of them is speaking at this moment over the Level 5 radio, which has been taken over by the rebels. The leaders have been executed, he says. They were hanged. They would have died anyway, but the rebels wanted to make a distinction, he says—"to kill the criminals in a way appropriate for criminals".

The executioner was a retired general. A famous commander of an armoured division. He is going to make a speech. I will try to write down what he says.

"Friends, citizens on all surviving Levels! Especially you comrades-in-arms on Levels 6 and 7. I have just hanged the arch-war-criminals, the so-called political leaders of our country. They were leaders, indeed: they led us to complete destruction.

"The trouble with them, friends, was that they did not trust us old, experienced and—I may add without false modesty— brave soldiers. In my day I led our country to victory on many occasions, with good fighting men to command and

163

good weapons to give them. In we went, destroying, killing, conquering. Some of us were wounded; some of us were killed; but the others survived to reap with their country the fruits of victory. Even the politicians got some glory for themselves out of it.

"But they did not trust those well-tried methods. Good guns and tanks, and good men too—those were not enough for them. They wanted rockets, robots, electronics and all those other outlandish devices.

"Now *we*, my friends, *we* are paying for it. But I hope it will comfort you to know that they did not get away with it. They were not allowed to die their fine electronic—or whatever the damned thing is called—their fine electronic death. They were hanged, with a rope, in the good old-fashioned way. I did it. And I may say I enjoyed doing it.

"Long live our Army. Long live our country. Long live . . ."

That is as far as he got, for he started vomiting violently.

SEPTEMBER 19

The news from Level 5 is confused and confusing. They seem to be playing politics right to the end. No wonder, I suppose, with so many politicians there, along with the top level of the *élite*—the cream of the cream.

But no more speeches from the retired general. He does not feel well enough. His place as 'head of the government' (whatever that may mean now) has been taken by a retired Air Force commander.

He made a speech this morning, one very much like the general's. He spoke warmly of wars fought by pilots in conventional aircraft. "As long as there were pilots flying the planes," he said, "it made no essential difference whether the planes were screw-propelled or jets, whether they flew at 200 m.p.h. or at supersonic speeds. But the moment those guided

164

missiles appeared—especially those devilish ground-to-ground intercontinental rockets—civilisation was doomed. No more glory for men, no more brave combats in the air, no more bombing of cities and installations by men who knew what they were about. But dehumanised war, automatic war, and its inevitable result: the end of civilisation."

This speaker was as eloquent as his predecessor, but he had to stop even before he arrived at 'Long live the Air Force'—stopped by an attack of nausea, we were told.

Oddly enough, until now I have never devoted much thought to the problem of war. Though war was my business, and though I underwent many tests and extensive training, or what appeared to be training, before I qualified as a push-button officer, I never thought beyond those buttons.

Was it the same with the soldier who drove a tank or pulled the trigger of a rifle? And what about the men who swung swords against an enemy they could actually grapple with?

I do not think I could be a swordsman. I could not kill with a club or a bayonet or a knife, let alone with my bare hands. But pushing a button—that was a different matter.

It has become so easy to destroy and kill. With a push-button a child, an innocent baby, could do it. In a sense, I suppose, the idea that the present disaster happened because war became dehumanised may have something in it.

But not more than something. For if it is wicked to destroy the world and wipe out the whole of humanity, thousands of millions, why is it good to kill ten million people and destroy just some parts of the world, as those old-style soldiers and airmen did?

Or is it *good* to kill with bows and arrows, because it is *evil* to kill with atomic bombs?

Surely not. Either it is good to kill, and then to kill off humanity is good; or it is evil to kill, in which case killing with any weapons is wrong.

It might well be that as the technology of war progressed, a different type of person did the killing. The head-hunter might have made a bad button-pusher, and the button-pusher a poor infantryman. But killing is killing, whatever way it is done. Once you allow the death of one person, the way is open for the massacre of a million.

And yet, and yet—the development of the atomic rocket did make a difference. A merely technical difference, perhaps, but with results . . . results which go far beyond technology.

There is a difference between limited destruction and total annihilation.

SEPTEMBER 20

They seem to be doomed—all of them. All three levels, 3, 4 and 5.

In some shelters the sickness has entered its final stages, in others it is not so far advanced. But according to our medical experts it is only a matter of time: the severity and universality of the symptoms make it quite clear that the civilian levels do not have long to live.

And they know it. But they cannot do anything about it. They wait for their caves to turn into mass graves.

All this has happened so quickly. It is strange that the water supplies of all the different shelters became poisoned at roughly the same time. Within the short space of three days the sickness had spread throughout the three levels.

How this happened is hard to explain. Perhaps all the shelters were built in geologically similar areas, in places where the ground was fairly soft. To dig deep shelters through rock would have been very difficult. It could have been done given plenty of time, but time was short. And perhaps it was not polluted rain water that penetrated and poisoned the water supplies of the shelters, but some capillary water in the ground.

166

Be that as it may, it happened. It happened quickly and on all three civilian levels.

Levels 6 and 7 seem to be safe. The experts say so. The shelters are deep enough for the filtering process to do its work. Even so, their water supplies are regularly checked for possible radioactivity. If this had been done on the higher levels, they might have been able to take precautions in time, though the job of distilling enough water for everybody without the proper equipment, would have been almost impossible. People would probably have died from thirst. One of the broadcasts received today said that on Level 4 some people had given up hope of getting enough clean water and were quenching their thirst with the freely flowing supply of poison.

I dare say they have given up trying to purify the water now. It is too late to do any good. And probably there is nobody left to work their makeshift distilleries.

SEPTEMBER 21

Broadcasts from the civilian levels are few and far between. They do not care whether we are fully informed or not. Or else it is hard to find anyone to operate the transmitter. Whatever the reason, they are mostly silent.

It is curious how this radioactive death silences people even before the life actually leaves their bodies. Though perhaps death usually works that way.

But what is the difference? They are fated to die. Some went yesterday, some are going today. More will go tomorrow and the day after. Supposing some survive for another week or two? That will not be life. Just an extended agony.

So the world is shrinking once again. Our part of it used to have about 622,500 inhabitants. Soon the number will be down to 2,500.

Death works fast. In a second it can kill a man, a thousand

men, a million men. A thousand millions it can kill in one second. The pushing of a button can do it.

Perhaps I exaggerate: in the deep caves, radioactive death comes more slowly. But it comes just as surely.

SEPTEMBER 22

This morning we picked up a radio message from the enemy suggesting that we should conclude a peace treaty. It also informed us that the entire civilian population over there, including the government and its various officials, is gone. They were all killed at one time or another by blast, fire or, finally, radiation. All that is left is the military level—about a thousand people, self-sufficient for centuries.

As a reason for making peace they pointed out that there was no longer anything to dispute: no territory, no strategic positions, no wealth, no markets, no uncommitted areas— nothing. "And," they added, "peaceful relations may add some fun to life underground, which is not very interesting."

So the enemy's lot is similar to ours. We have not been told exactly what their system of shelters was, but they are all graves except for the military one, which must correspond to our Level 7. Our enemy has shrunk even more than we!

And now we should make peace for the fun of it. As good a reason as any, though it is the queerest political motive I have ever struck!

After lunch today we were told that our radio staff were trying to get in touch with Level 5. They were asking for instructions.

On Level 7 there is no recognised authority to decide matters of such moment as peace treaties. We waged the war at the command of a gadget, except for the two orders which had to be given locally for purely military reasons. We could

have been told what to do by the political leaders on Level 5—
who may *still* be able to give us orders. Not the same leaders,
of course, but the men who hanged them.

Level 7's internal affairs are managed on Level 7, naturally. Our own administrative officers deal with such things
as timetables for the use of the lounge, marriage arrangements
and so forth. But they cannot take any political responsibility.

So we are trying to get instructions from Level 5. They may
have heard the enemy's radio message themselves, of course,
though it was addressed to "Our comrades in push-button
war on the other side of the globe". That is why we have taken
the initiative in the matter of the peace treaty—in case Level 5
does not take it.

SEPTEMBER 23

No, Level 5 does nothing about it. They have not replied at
all. Perhaps they cannot. There are no authorities left, maybe,
or nobody to receive radio messages.

Somebody on Level 6 or 7 will have to make the decision.
But who?

The general loudspeaker system has just announced that
Level 7's three chief administrators have decided to hold a
referendum. The peace treaty question is to be decided by a
majority vote. A truly democratic answer.

Voters are instructed to press a red button, identify themselves and say whether or not they want peace. Level 6 will
be asked to participate, of course, their votes being added to
the democratic pool.

I am in favour of peace, and I intend to record my vote as
soon as I have finished writing this entry. I am sure most people will feel the same way. Down here on Level 7, at least.
I do not know how Level 6 will react. Up there they are *defensive* button-pushers, and I have no idea what kind of char-

169

acter was looked for when they were selected. They may be very different from ourselves, which makes their views on peace hard to guess. We shall just have to wait and see what they say.

Level 6 is silent. Last night, and again this morning, our people broadcast the voting arrangements and asked Level 6 for their comments. But they did not even acknowledge the receipt of our message.

This is most curious, for physically they are the nearest to us of all the shelters. Our transmitter has been checked and found to be functioning properly. Presumably something has gone wrong with theirs.

In the meantime we have informed the enemy that consultations are going on concerning their peace proposals.

Level 6 is still silent. Like the grave.

There must be something seriously wrong there. It cannot be just a matter of the transmitter. PBY Command, with its team of specialists trained to operate, check and repair the most complicated electronic gadgets, would be the last to be silenced by the breakdown of a radio transmitter.

More and more people down here are saying that Level 6 has perished. Probably so suddenly that they did not even have time to broadcast the news.

But what could have happened there? Perhaps their atomic reactor exploded—if this is possible. Perhaps the plants suddenly died and left people with no air to breathe. Perhaps. . . .

Who can know what really happened? No one has lived

long enough in the caves to know all the things that can go wrong. It is impossible to anticipate everything. Though we knew how aircraft worked, there were still crashes. Railways had been operated even longer, but that did not prevent the occasional accident.

So why should we be surprised if a shelter perishes, even one which looks completely safe? Look at what sometimes happened to submarines. And what are our levels but subterraneans?

Why should we consider ourselves so completely safe? Just because the surface is so fatally dangerous?

SEPTEMBER 26

We have just about given up trying to get an answer out of Level 6. It is generally assumed that they are dead, though even the scare-mongers of yesterday are too awed by what this means to talk about it openly any more. But you can read people's thoughts in their faces. This seems to touch our level more closely than anything which has happened before. If it is possible for a shelter, a deep shelter with its own energy and air supplies, to go out like a light, for no apparent reason— then anything can happen.

So people here are losing their sense of security. Some are looking distinctly nervous. Even X-107m, who has developed a tic at the left-hand corner of his mouth.

Until now the feeling has been: "We are safe. We are deep in the earth. We are the most privileged, the chosen few who have survived and will go on living."

The feeling creeping in now is: "Shall we survive? Are we not just the last to die, waiting longer than the others for our turn to come? How soon shall we perish? *How* shall we perish? From plant decay and lack of oxygen? From some trouble we cannot even diagnose? Shall we know that we are dying, or will the blow be sudden and catch us unawares?"

We have concluded a peace treaty with the enemy. The voting was almost unanimously in favour of it. Why not? We may as well enjoy some live company before we join the other levels.

I wrote that paragraph this morning. Since then I have been thinking what a strange peace this is which we have made. A peace of death.

We are at peace not because the world is united, physically or in spirit, but because the warring camps are separated by an insurmountable barrier of death.

We, our former enemy and ourselves, wanted to be masters of mankind. Each of us wanted to rule the whole world, or to save it (both formulas amount to the same thing now). And the result: both sides have been diminished to a few hundred cave-dwellers.

Never in all human history was there anything so grotesque. Two vast countries, the two greatest world powers, reduced in a matter of hours to the status of a few moles, hiding below ground in the constant fear that the next hour will be their last.

There is some mutual entertainment on the air. We and our ex-enemy are exchanging slogans which express ideals supposedly justifying the war. The entertainment value lies in the fact that we both look on the funny side of it. The ironical exchanges carry on in this fashion:

"Cave-men of the world, unite!"

"Freedom and democracy for all cave-men!"

"True, people's democracy for all cave-men!"

"Let's make the world safe for the cave-men!"

"Equality for cave-men!"

"Freedom of speech for cave-men!"

"A classless society of cave-men!"

"A real democracy of cave-men!"

And so on. The more high-sounding the slogan, the hollower it rings—and the more people laugh at it. Our ex-enemy seems to enjoy the game as much as we do. We have been invited by the general loudspeaker to send in slogans of our own to be broadcast. I have submitted mine: "At last the world is united".

SEPTEMBER 29

My slogan went out this morning.

Their reply was rather slow in coming, and when it arrived I was not at all sure whether they intended it to be funny: "But it lives in separate shelters."

I was asked whether I wanted to answer this one, and after thinking about it for a while I submitted my answer: "But it dies the one death."

This time their reply came back in a flash: "Divided we live, united we die!"

SEPTEMBER 30

I spent this afternoon writing a short story for a possible broadcast. Here it is.

Once upon a time there were two friends called A and B. They had known each other for years and used to spend a great deal of time together. Even when A had found himself a girl friend, and B had found himself a girl friend, the two of them still enjoyed each other's company so much that they used to go out with their girl friends together. But they were not at all alike to look at. A wore his hair smooth and sleekly shining, and his girl said she liked it that way; while B's hair stuck up like the spines of a porcupine, which was the style his girl favoured.

Each of them preferred his own hair-cut and did not approve of the style which seemed to please the other one's girl friend, but for a long time both were reluctant to say so. Then one day A said to B, in the friendliest way: "Look here, my friend, I do think it would be so much better if you cut your hair my way." And B replied: "Since you mention it, I've often thought your hair would look much better cut like mine."

To begin with they discussed the relative merits and demerits of the two styles most amicably. But when each saw that the other had no intention of changing his mind, the argument began to grow heated.

When A got back home one day, he looked for the largest pair of scissors he could find and laid them ready for the morrow.

And when B got home, he too set aside the biggest pair of scissors he possessed.

Next day, when the two friends met, they brandished their scissors and flew at each other's heads, paying no attention to their girl friends' protesting cries. Before you could say *snip*, there they were, standing horrified at the sight of each other's bald head, and gingerly feeling the place where their own hair had been.

While the two girl friends said: "I could never love a man with a bald head"—and ran off down the road as fast as they could go.

OCTOBER 1

My story was broadcast this morning. People liked it. It went down well with the other side too, and they broadcast a humorous retort: "Buy yourself a wig, bald fellow!"

My reply was: "There are no wigs to be had underground. We shall have to stay bald."

No, not everything that is gone can be replaced. A bald head is bald—even with a wig. A destroyed world is destroyed.

OCTOBER 2

Now our ex-enemy's broadcasts have stopped. Maybe it is just a technical hitch. But maybe—no, it is better not to think about it. Let us wait and see.

X-107m and P seem to get along well. I do not see P often, as I prefer not to go to the lounge, while she seldom visits her husband in our room. But X-107m appears very satisfied with his lot.

He does not keep me company in quite the way he did before. I listen to music more now, even though the tape has repeated itself many times since our arrival here. The same thing every twelve days. But, even so, there is something about a piece of quality which enables you to listen to it again and again.

OCTOBER 3

They are silent. They must have died. Suddenly, like Level 6. Perhaps from the same cause—the unknown one. We shall never know it, unless we perish the same way. And if we do, we shall not know it for long.

People on Level 7 are distressed, deeply distressed. I see around me the same long faces that marked the first days of our seclusion in these dungeons. People look quite as unhappy as they did before they became adjusted.

They feel lonely again. Not because of the seclusion, but because they are alone in the world. There is no longer even an ex-enemy to communicate with.

Also they are afraid. They fear gamma rays and neutrons, alpha particles and beta particles. They are afraid to eat and to drink and to breathe. But perhaps most of all they are afraid of the unknown. The fact that they do not know how and when they may be struck down makes them nervous. They are afraid to sleep, for they may never wake.

Spiritually, radiation is already active on Level 7. It spreads panic without even being here. This might be the most powerful form of psychological warfare. And the most effortless: nobody does anything, and the fear is universal. The idea of radiation enters the mind imperceptibly, just as the real radiation invisibly penetrates the body.

OCTOBER 4

The ex-enemy has been given up for dead. We *are* alone now, literally and absolutely alone.

How long shall we last? Shall we survive down here? Raise families? Keep humanity alive until one day man creeps out of these miserable holes?

Or shall we perish as the other levels did? And will we know what has hit us or not? Shall we be hit suddenly and unawares, or shall we have to watch death spreading all around us? Who knows?

The atomic reactor which supplies our energy has to undergo some repair work, so everything will come to a halt for an hour. I intend to stop writing and go to bed before they switch off the lighting. It will not inconvenience many people to be without light at this time of night. I expect most of them are asleep anyway. The others can discover what it is like to be as blind as real moles, which should be quite interesting.

OCTOBER 5

I was asleep last night long before the reactor was repaired. This morning I was told that the job took not one hour but three, and that there was an accident: one of the atomic energy officers working on it, AE-307m, suffered a very strong overdose of radiation and died before morning.

Like X-117, AE-307m was given a short obituary over the general loudspeaker system. "He gave his life to ensure our survival," the speaker said, and his praise of the dead man seemed to me quite fair. With no reactor we should last a very short time indeed!

It is a sad business, this. Everybody feels sorry for AE-307m. And for his widow.

OCTOBER 6

The two AE officers who helped AE-307m repair the reactor have died too.

Moreover, I saw somebody vomiting today at lunch. Quite a few others left the dining-room hurriedly during the meal. Has it started?

OCTOBER 7

It has finally reached us. We shall not get away with it. Sickness and death are all around. Some people die with

177

hardly a struggle. Others only vomit to start with, and manage to keep going. Slight nausea is all I have felt so far.

And the funny part about it is that it is the reactor—our own atomic reactor—which is killing us. The source of life down here, our man-made sun, now sends its death-dealing rays through Level 7.

Before long we shall all be gone. This is the beginning of the end.

OCTOBER 8

This morning the loudspeaker gave some official information about the source of trouble.

Something went wrong with the reactor. If it had happened on the surface the reactor could have been stopped, isolated and repaired at leisure. If necessary, people could have been moved to a safe distance. But here on Level 7 there was no choice. The reactor had to be repaired where it was, and quickly, even with the danger of lethal radiation. Without light, the plants would have stopped supplying oxygen; and we would soon have died.

So the AE officers risked their lives and partly succeeded: the energy supply will continue. Unfortunately, so will the lethal radiation. The reactor will go on working simultaneously as a source of life and a source of death.

Precisely how and why, I do not know. And I do not care. There are some 'technical reasons'. That is enough explanation for me. It seems to be enough for others too.

OCTOBER 9

This death is quick. We must be getting powerful doses of those rays or particles—whatever is killing us.

People are dying all round like flies. Yesterday some at-

178

tempt was still being made to remove the corpses, but today nobody seems to be bothering, and the bodies lie where they fall. Perhaps there is no one from the medical department left to take them away, or nobody strong enough. Most people do not come out of their rooms even for meals. I only went out for lunch today, and the sight of half a dozen corpses in the dining-room very nearly stopped me eating. Quite two thirds of the meals on the moving band were left untouched.

Although I do not feel as bad as the others, I know it cannot last. Death is in me.

X-107m has just come into the room. He looks very pale, and has flopped down on his bed.

He has just told me that P died about half an hour ago. He was with her at the end, and he says she mentioned me. He is not sure whether she was conscious or delirious.

"She was a fine woman," he says.

OCTOBER 10

Level 7 is emptying fast. I went out for lunch again just now, and the place looked like a battlefield. Corpses scattered around everywhere. But not a wound to be seen.

The loudspeaker has been silent today. Presumably nobody is left to operate it any more.

X-107m died just a few minutes ago. He is lying on his bed. He will have to stay there, for there is nobody to take him away and I have not the strength to do it.

He was not talkative during his delirium. But sometime late this afternoon he called me over and pointed to his jacket. When I carried it across to him he groped in a pocket for a piece of paper, which he gave me, just managing to say: "Into the diary."

179

On the sheet of paper I found what appears to be some sort of poetry, though it is very irregular and has no rhymes. I shall copy it into my diary now, since he asked me to, not that anybody will ever read it. Or the diary.

This is what he wrote:

When I was a boy I used to watch my sister build a house
    of cards.
One on another balanced in delicate equilibrium
(Quiet now, don't knock the table)
Until there the house stood, tall and fine.

But I was mischievous,
I liked to blow the house down,
To watch the cards slip, the house crumble and fall.
To destroy what had been built was my pleasure.
Just one puff, and all that labour of careful construction—
Nothing!

When I grew up I found that houses were not made of cards.
Plaster, concrete, wood, steel.
I could blow my lungs out
And not shift those in a thousand thousand years.

But something could. Progress had seen to it. Puff!—
And the plaster, the concrete, the wood and the steel
Blown by the bomb's breath
Tumble like cards.
In this game atoms are trumps.

And it's easy, so easy.
Just push the button with your finger, lightly,
And down go the office blocks, down go the factories,
Houses, churches, all monuments of man's endeavour,
Down like a pack of cards!

I never suspected X-107m of writing strange stuff like that. What did he want to say? Just to explain the psychology of his push-button career? Or to indict himself? Did he feel any remorse? He didn't show it ever.

Who knows? I almost added "Who cares?" But *I* care! He was a fine fellow, and a good comrade too.

I have grown terribly thin and weak. I managed to crawl as far as the dining-room at lunch time today, but by the time I had got there the sight and smell of the dead bodies (some have been lying around for three days now) quite took away my feeble appetite. I rested for a few minutes, hoping I should meet someone there to talk to. But nobody came. Nobody!

I did not see a living person today. For all I know I may now be the last man alive on earth. And I shall be the last to die. A distinction in the midst of extinction!

It is strangely ironical that we, PBX Command, should be killed by a gadget making a peaceful use of atomic energy. It does not seem fair. Divine justice, I always thought, was eye for eye, tooth for tooth. It should be bomb for bomb. Instead we are being killed by a piece of faulty machinery. Not really a warrior's death.

Perhaps God intends it as a sort of joke. "You killed with bombs," He says. "You will be killed by peaceful radiation."

Or maybe He is a Christian God, and Christian charity inspires His acts: "You killed with atomic missiles," He says, "but I shall help you over to the other side with a reactor."

What am I talking about? God? Reactor? I feel hot, hot and cold. I think I had better get into bed, if I can still climb up to that top bunk. I cannot move X-107.

181

I feel I am dying. I am glad I brought my diary up here when I got into bed last night. I am so very weak. I hardly feel a thing, except pains. I must rest for a while.

I am dying, and the world is dying with me. I am the last man on earth, the sole surviving specimen of homo sapiens. *Sapiens* indeed!

It is lonely here. I wish I had someone to talk to. Even a dying soldier deserted on the battlefield cannot have felt as lonely as I feel. He had his comrades to think of, his family— people he was dying for, or thought he was dying for. But I have nobody to die for. Nobody to think of. They are all dead. No one outside, no one in the ex-enemy shelter, no one on Level 7.

Does everybody feel as lonely as this when he dies? I wonder if it makes any difference to have family and friends around you. I wish I had.

I would give anything to have some people around me! The only face I can see belongs to the clock on the wall.

But I can listen to some music—I can just reach the switch if I stretch my arm far enough.

Done! Beethoven's 'Eroica'. It sounds wonderful. Even now. Is it human or divine? It will last longer than I shall, longer than humanity. If that reactor does not break down again the tape will go on playing for years. In twelve days' time, when I am dead, the 'Eroica' will sound in this room again. In twenty-four days' time too, in thirty-six, in forty-eight. . . . And outside the sun will rise and set with no one there to watch it.

I am dying, and humanity dies with me. I am the dying

humanity. But let the tape revolve, let the music last. I do not know why, but I want *something* to last.

I have been sick again. It has left me very weak. I can hardly keep the pen from slipping out of my fingers.

I must stay conscious. Like in that nightmare. I have to. For my sake. For humanity's sake. I am the last creature alive. I must go on living. Let the music go on, and let me listen. But I feel faint.

I think I must have passed out. The clock seems to have moved very fast. It is now 16.00 hours. Four o'clock in the afternoon. The music still goes on. It will go on for ever.

It makes me feel worse, thinking about it. I am going to die. Why should anything go on when I am dead? That music—why should that outlive me? What is the point of music that nobody can hear? I shall turn it off.

It is no good. I tried, and I could not reach the switch. So it will go on playing. It is a funny thought, that. All right, let the tape revolve.

I do not think I can write any more. But I must try hard. This is my contact with—with what was.

Sunshine was. Does the sun still shine?

I cannot read the clock across the room. But it is still light. No. Dark.

I cannot see Oh friends people mother sun

I   I

Afterword

by H. Bruce Franklin

How wonderful it would be if *Level 7* were some outdated fiction, which we could read comfortably as a curious relic of its times. But, alas, the thirty years that have passed since the novel's first publication have made it ever less dated, ever more plausible—and ever more terrifying.

When *Level 7* was published back in 1959, few readers could have taken its nightmare vision very literally. After all, our frenzied quest for "security" was still a long way from attaining today's global doomsday machine, capable of annihilating all civilization on earth and possibly exterminating the human species. Almost all the nuclear weapons of the United States were still carried by manned bombers based hours from their targets and subject to recall long after being launched. Just becoming operational were the first few Intercontinental Ballistic Missiles (ICBMs), immune to recall once launched and able to strike the Soviet Union in less time than it took to heat a TV dinner. On the Soviet side, it was not until several months before *Level 7's* publication that the USSR finally produced even a few vehicles with sufficient range to attack the continental United States with nuclear weapons. It would be eight years before Mutual Assured Destruction (MAD) would become the official "defense" strategy of the United States. And the most advanced computers in the world then were less powerful than the personal computers in many of today's homes. So *Level 7's* push-button apocalypse was still just a novelist's surrealistic fantasy.

Yet Roshwald's novel was hailed immediately as an eloquent prophecy of the suicidal outcome latent in the nuclear arms race. J.B. Priestley called *Level 7* "easily the most powerful attack on the whole nuclear madness that any creative writer has made so far." Linus Pauling described it as "the most realistic picture of nuclear war that I have ever read in any work of fiction." And Bertrand Russell pleaded for it to be "read by every adult in both

185

the Eastern and Western blocs.'' The *New York Herald Tribune* declared that if these adults were to heed Russell's plea, ''the world might literally be saved.''[1]

Indeed the novel has been read widely and avidly. Its English-language editions went through printing after printing, selling over 400,000 copies by 1980. It was translated into Dutch, French, Italian, German, Spanish, Swedish, Rumanian, Norwegian, and Japanese. Television adaptations were broadcast in Great Britain and Australia. Its worldwide audience has continued to expand, with translations into such languages as Chinese (1984) and Hungarian (1988). Yet in 1981, *Level 7* was taken out of print in North America, just as its most deranged schemes were being implemented.

This was one year after President Jimmy Carter issued Presidential Directive 59, which officially ordered U.S. forces to prepare for a protracted and ''flexible'' nuclear war, as opposed to the previously declared policy of nuclear deterrence. Simultaneously with the disappearance of *Level 7,* President Reagan issued NSDD 13, which proclaimed that the goal of U.S. policy is to ''prevail'' in a protracted nuclear war.[2] The emerging policy of developing ''the ability to wage nuclear war rationally'' had been explained in 1980 by Colin Gray, soon to be one of the Reagan Administration's top nuclear policy strategists:

> The United States should plan to defeat the Soviet Union and to do so at a cost that would not prohibit U.S. recovery. Washington should identify war aims that in the last resort would contemplate the destruction of Soviet political authority and the emergence of a postwar world order compatible with Western values.[3]

Or, as the government explains to the destroyers of humanity on Level 7: ''You . . . serve as the advance guard of our country, our creed, our way of life . . . . You are the defenders of truth and justice'' (12).

Indeed, it seems that perhaps the leaders of our government had read *Level 7*—but as a blueprint rather than as a warning. The standard arrangement of the button pushers in our missile silos today is precisely that described by X-127: "the system will only work if two people push the same button at the same time"; "the two controls are far enough apart to stop one man pushing both the buttons at once"; "my colleagues and I do not decide when to push the button, or which one to push. Our job is just to keep watch and, if and when the time comes, to do what the loudspeaker tells us" (21). While you read these words, teams just like this are underground, temporarily sealed off from any information about the world, except for possible orders to destroy it, which would be transmitted to them electronically. The North American Defense Command, along with its master computer whose analysis is central to our destiny, is buried deep under Cheyenne Mountain in Colorado. Just as in the novel, a presumed nuclear attack on the United States could lead to the activation of robot transmitters (the Emergency Rocket Communications System, MN-16525C) programmed to order all U.S. nuclear forces to launch their weapons.[4]

X-127 and his fellow button pushers are selected according to a psychological profile assuring their willingness to destroy all life on Earth. When they have doubts about performing this task, they are considered mentally sick and must undergo therapy designed to cure them of their conscience. The real-life counterparts of these fictional button pushers are represented by Lieutenant Steven Gifford, formerly a missile-launch officer in training. Gifford was shocked to learn that he would be expected to carry out U.S. contingency plans for first-strike attacks and thermonuclear annihilation of large civilian population centers, which the Pentagon euphemistically refers to as "flexibility targeting." He was told that firing missiles should be a "Pavlovian reaction" regardless of the target or situation, and that he "should salivate at the very thought of turning the missile key." When Gifford declared "I'm not a robot," and indicated that he wouldn't push the button without thinking about it first, he was sent to a psychiatrist. The Air Force then gave him a less than honorable discharge, even though his "only problem," according to testimony by both the psychiatrist and the base chaplain, "was an active conscience."[5]

What form of literature or art can adequately describe a world where conscience is a disease, the highest level of human existence is the lowest underground, where "not only perfect democracy but also absolute freedom" consists of mindlessly following orders by machines, and the supreme purpose of society is to design weapons and train people to exterminate the human species? Five years before Stanley Kubrick's *Dr. Strangelove, Or, How I Learned to Stop Worrying and Love the Bomb,* Mordecai Roshwald's *Level 7* was the first major work to recognize that the nuclear arms race is too demonically absurd to be adequately dramatized in the form of realism.

The novel's surrealistic future comes very close to projecting what Jonathan Schell in *The Fate of the Earth* calls unimaginable: the extinction by nuclear war of all human consciousness.[6] Roshwald achieves this by showing the obliteration of human consciousness as not merely what would happen *after* a nuclear holocaust but as the historical process necessary to make such a literally inhuman act possible. Thus X-127 and his cohorts have already ceased to be human beings even before they descend into the depths of the earth, and in this sense they are truly "the advance guard of our country, our creed, our way of life." For a society that designs and deploys the machinery necessary to destroy our species has already become so militarized and bureaucratized that its ideal citizens must be unconscious automatons incapable of feeling love for humanity or remorse for its annihilation.

X-127 himself soon becomes aware that "I was incapable of love; and so was everyone else here" (55), and after it is too late he realizes "how dead" he had been "inside" (155). His most intimate personal relationship is his brief marriage to P-867m, the intensity of which is well expressed in these words of tenderness and passion:

> We smiled when we saw how our names had grown, and decided on the spot that between ourselves we would forget the ponderous P-867m and X-127m and call each other P and X for short. (86)

As he watches the electronic images of the devastation he has launched, his only emotional experience is entertainment by the bright colors:

> Aesthetically the picture was quite pleasing. Red blobs and blue and yellow spots, some on the red blobs and some outside them. (118)

He is like some ultimate player in a video arcade, which President Ronald Reagan, two weeks before his 1983 Star Wars speech, celebrated as a splendid training instrument for the nation's future warriors: ". . . . watch a 12-year-old take evasive action and score multiple hits while playing 'Space Invaders.'"[7]

It is perhaps revealing that the great majority of students to whom I have taught *Level 7* assume that its characters and locale are American. Roshwald is extremely careful to provide no indication of whether the novel is set in the United States or the Soviet Union,[8] implying that the two rival nuclear superpowers are transforming themselves into monstrous mirror images of each other, and suggesting to the reader: if the shoe fits wear it. Is our metamorphosis become so grotesque that we have trouble distinguishing ourselves from Roshwald's nightmare?

That question leads to others, perhaps equally troubling. For *Level 7* insinuates that the nuclear monster we have created, like Victor Frankenstein's hideous creature, is itself an expression of the character of its creator. And it was the United States that devised and used the first atomic bombs, and then initiated the nuclear arms race that has so radically transformed human existence on this planet. Viewed in this light, the novel may indeed be holding a satirist's mirror up to the features of the time and place in which it was written: the United States of America in the 1950s.

My own sense that this was one main thrust of *Level 7* was confirmed in a letter that Roshwald sent to me in response to a query about what led to his writing the book. He explained that he wrote the first draft in 1957, in Minneapolis, shortly after coming to this country, and that "besides the obvious concern, perhaps subconsciously, I also wanted to convey my sense of isolation and alienation in the new setting of America."

189

> The reliance on technology and the penchant for gadgets,
> the self-sufficient hotels with all the stores and services
> provided in one huge building, the ubiquitous interchange-
> able smiles and crew-cuts, the predictable exchanges on
> the weather and other small talk, the avoidance of any con-
> troversial discussion—all that was new to me and seemed
> to point to a uniformly happy, efficient and self-sufficient
> society, verging on automata or robots.[9]

Roshwald's then describes the shocking experience that brought all this home to him: "When I assigned a class of mine at the University of Minnesota to read *Brave New World,* some of my students thought that Huxley intended to depict a perfect society and they liked it."

Even without this hint, it should be clear that *Level 7* is a dystopia in the same tradition as *Brave New World.* And like Huxley's novel it participates in the epic encounter between utopian and anti-utopian conceptions that, extending back all the way to Plato's *Republic,* now underlies crucial ideological struggles of modern times. Indeed, the novel's eloquence as a warning against the nuclear arms race has tended to obscure its magnificent achieve-ment as part of this literary tradition. Eventually, I believe, Rosh-wald's remorseless apocalypse will be recognized as one of the masterpieces of anti-utopian literature. For *Level 7* shows how the worst social nightmares of the twentieth century, developing in the specific historical form of the nuclear arms race, reach their insanely logical culmination.

The surrealistic landscape of *Level 7* twists or inverts familiar features of the utopian-dystopian terrain. From the *Republic* come new versions of the Allegory of the Cave, of arguments about the ideal state, and of Plato's Guardian warriors, who would be taught as children by invented myths that all their indoctrination was a mere dream, that "in reality they were the whole time down inside the earth, being moulded and fostered while their arms and all their equipment were being fashioned also."[10] The novel's dehumanizing underground machinery has roots in E. M. Forster's 1909 novella *The Machine Stops* and the 1926 film *Metropolis.*

The allegedly perfectly rational society—which is actually based on the most profound irrationality—crowns a Russian tradition stretching from Fyodor Dostoevsky through Valery Briusov's 1905 novella *The Republic of the Southern Cross* to Yevgeny Zamiatin's 1920 novel *We,* whose citizens also have numbers for names. Once recognized, the reverberations from *Brave New World* and George Orwell's *1984* ring loud and clear.

Unlike most earlier anti-utopias, however, *Level 7* locates the menace to humanity not in "human nature" but in a very specific historical phenomenon: the nuclear arms race, that ultimate form of institutional, cultural, technological, psychological, and ethical alienation. Indeed, despite its relentlessly dark vision of where we may be heading, *Level 7* ends by affirming humanity, life, and love. And its comic undercurrents assume an audience that shares the very values denied by this grotesque, humorless parody of modern society. Even X-127 awakens, though of course too late, to his bonds to "friends people mother sun." By asking us to recognize Level 7 for what it is—the reign of anti-humanism incarnate in our cult of "defense"—Roshwald's novel implies that we have the potential to overcome the external and internal forces now threatening to transform us from social beings who thrive on love into mindless, robotic, genocidal button pushers.

1. J. B. Priestley, "Best Anti-Bomb Story Yet," *Reynolds News,* September 20, 1959; Luther Nichols, "A Pushbutton Annihilation," *San Francisco Examiner,* April 12, 1960; Gouverneur Paulding, "Searing Tale Envisions the End of the Life We Know," *New York Herald Tribune Book Review,* March 6, 1960.

2. Robert Scheer, *With Enough Shovels: Reagan, Bush and Nuclear War* (New York: Random House, 1982), p. 12.

3. Colin S. Gray and Keith Payne, "Victory Is Possible," *Foreign Policy* 39 (Summer 1980), pp. 14-27; reprinted in Donna Gregory, ed., *The Nuclear Predicament* (New York: St. Martin's Press, 1986), pp. 115-23.

4. See H. Bruce Franklin, *War Stars: The Superweapon and the American Imagination* (New York: Oxford University Press, 1988), 207, for a discussion of this doomsday apparatus and how its existence was disclosed.

5. Jack Anderson, "AF Shows No Conscience in Drumming Out Missileman," (Newark) *Star-Ledger,* March 16, 1983.

6. Jonathan Schell, *The Fate of the Earth* (New York: Avon, 1982), p. 138.

7. "Reagan Says Video Games Provide the Right Stuff," *Wall Street Journal,* March 9, 1983.

8. All previous U.S. editions contain a single phrase suggesting an American locale: "Our attitude probably resembled that of a bunch of *Ivy-league college boys . . . .*" When I pointed this out to the author, he was dumbfounded, for he was certain that he had meticulously avoided the slightest detail locating the action in either the United States or the Soviet Union. He then discovered that the phrase had been inserted without his knowledge or authorization as an editorial revision of the first edition, published in England, which read: "Our attitude probably resembled that of a bunch of aristocratic officer-cadets."

9. Letter to me from Mordecai Roshwald, September 15, 1988.

10. *The Republic of Plato,* translated by Francis Cornford (NY: Oxford University Press, 1945), p. 106.